DARLIA SAWYER

A Captive Heart

By Darlia Sawyer

Copyright © 2019
Written by: Darlia Sawyer
Published by: Forget Me Not Romances, a division of Winged Publications

This book is a work of fiction. Names, characters, places, and incidents are the product of the author's imagination and are used fictitiously. Any resemblance to actual events, locales, or persons, living or dead, is coincidental.

All rights reserved.

ISBN-13: 979-8-3493-0416-3

Psalm 50:15

Call upon Me in the day of trouble;
I shall rescue you, and you will honor Me.

Acknowledgment

God is ever present in our lives and it is only because of His faithfulness I have been able to write.

As always a big thank you to my husband, Ken. Without your help I would be lost. Love you forever.

This book is dedicated to the women who were with me in the beginning of my writing journey. Two of them have gone on to be with our Lord. Sharon Bridgewater and Muriel Morley, you are both missed more than you know and I will forever be thankful for all you poured into me. Patti Hill, you are an amazing teacher and writer. I'm thankful for all you've done to help writers know what is essential in excelling in their craft.

.

Chapter One

1898 Texas

Goosebumps rose on Ella's arms as hoof beats vibrated the ground beneath her. She turned in her saddle to face the commotion as a lasso fell past her shoulders and tightened around her middle. Adrenaline coursed through her veins as thoughts of her mother's kidnapping flashed through her mind. Panicked, she kicked her horse in the sides hoping to put distance between herself and the assailant.

The rope reached its end, jerking her off the rear of the horse. The impact on the packed soil knocked the wind from her lungs. Gasping for air she struggled to yell but nothing came out.

The man jumped off his horse and raced to her. "Are you hurt? I wanted to bring you to a slow stop."

Ella gulped air as she tried to talk. "You chased me down and lassoed me. How can you claim you weren't trying to hurt me?"

"I'm a private investigator hired by your mother to take you to Colorado. I hope you'll come without any trouble, but either way, we're going to Cripple Creek." The man lifted his hat and raked his fingers through his long black hair.

"I don't know who hired you, but it wasn't my mother. I won't go anywhere with you! My mother is deceased, so you need to go back and inform this woman, I'm not her daughter." Ella turned her head, hoping to see someone traveling down the road. She had to get free.

"Whoever told you your mother is dead, lied? I assure you she's alive. She hired the best private detectives to locate you, and all roads led here. Once you meet her you will be amazed at the resemblance. You're a younger version with the same red hair. I have a contract with her and I must take you there to fulfill it." He put his arms around her waist and picked her up, then took the rope hanging from his belt and tied her hands behind her. Ella struggled to get free, but the rope held tight.

He put a rolled bandana into her mouth and tied it behind her head. Lifting her over his shoulder, he pushed her up onto the saddle of her horse. "Any more resistance from you, and I'll blindfold you too."

He grabbed her horse's reins, mounted his horse, and they trotted away from the road and the place she'd called home the last seven years. She already hated this woman who claimed to be her mother. If she wanted to meet her she should've come to Nacogdoches, not have her kidnapped.

~

It was a few hours past sunset when they stopped beside a narrow stream of water running alongside a wall of rock. There was a crevice in the wall which created a small cave. Her abductor held his hands up to help her down. Not wishing to touch him, she swung her leg over the other side of the saddle and slid off the horse. Ella's legs buckled, numb from riding so long. Her face smacked the dirt as she fell forward. She couldn't catch herself without the use of her hands. She needed to plan her moves better. She could've hit her head on a rock.

He grasped one of her arms and helped her to her feet. "Maybe, next time you'll let me help. You're lucky you didn't get hurt."

He untied the bandana and took it off. Dirt covered her face, and she tried to blink it from her eyes. The inside of her mouth felt like cotton. He took the lid off a canteen and brought it to her lips. Ella took a huge gulp, causing her to choke. The water dribbled from her mouth and down her dress but she didn't care. Nothing had ever tasted so wonderful.

"I'm sure you have matters to attend to. Remember we are miles from the closest town and you'd never make it there on foot without water and a gun for safety. I recognize you have no reason to believe me, but I'm not going to hurt you. I need to fulfill my contract and deliver you to your mother. I've never mistreated a woman, and I don't plan on starting with you. I will leave your hands untied if you'll cooperate." Ella nodded, and he cut the rope. She stumbled off toward the bushes.

"Stay in sight."

Light from the full moon illuminated the surrounding land. Her mind whirled as she contemplated scenarios that would lead to freedom, but none ended with her being alive. For now, she'd stay with him. She prayed his statements were true.

She'd have to keep her wits about her to recognize the right moment to escape. She finished up and walked back toward the horses. He gathered wood and put it inside the cave.

She kept her distance as he built a fire and spread blankets out on each side of it.

"My name is, Shane Wyatt. As I mentioned earlier, I'm a private investigator, not an outlaw. I don't make kidnapping people a habit. This is the first time I've taken someone against their will. I accepted this job because you were stolen from your mother as a baby. After hearing her story, I figured she deserved a chance to meet you. And to be quite honest, I need the money. I've fallen on hard times and this money will get me back on my feet."

"So that's how you justify the crime of kidnapping? I was not taken from my parents. My mother died and my father could not take care of me, so he left me at an orphanage. You've been lied too. This woman must have bad intentions if she'd lie to you about being my mother." Ella watched him set a small pan on the fire and empty a can of beans into it.

"I don't think she's lying. She knows too much about you and has spent a lot of money and time trying to find you. She has nothing to gain by this."

The smell emitting from the pan made Ella's stomach growl. She hadn't eaten since breakfast.

Thoughts of home and her family produced anguish so strong she winced.

"What's wrong? Did you hurt something when you fell off the horse?" Shane glanced up from the pan.

"I might never see my family again, and it hurt to even think those thoughts." Ella grabbed a blanket and wrapped it around her as she sat near the fire. "How do you know this woman has honest intentions? She may wish to keep me as a prisoner."

"I can't imagine she would do that. I reckon, she just needs to meet you and is hoping you'll want to have some type of relationship with her. If she decided to keep you there, I'd take you back to your family. The sooner we get to Cripple Creek, Colorado, and you see your mother, the sooner I'll get the money I need to pay off my debt. Then, you can go back to Texas." Shane pulled two plates from his bag and scooped the beans onto them. He handed one to Ella.

"Stop calling her my mother! Obviously, you don't understand right from wrong. I will fight you every step of the way if you continue to make me go to Colorado. I don't care if you need money to pay your debts. You call yourself a detective, but a better word would be criminal." Ella snatched the plate from his hand. She wanted to throw it at him but didn't know when she'd have more food, so she stuffed her anger and ate it.

"Sorry, Ella, I understand you don't want to go. However, we've got a long journey ahead of us. No matter what it takes, we're going to Cripple Creek, and I will hand you over to your mother. I understand why you don't think much of me. I hope, in time, you'll discover I'm not as bad as you assume."

Ella tossed her empty plate at him. "That day will never happen. I hope you hang when they find out you kidnapped me. My adopted father won't stop until he finds me."

Shane picked up their plates and the pan and left the cave. "You might want to get some sleep. We have a long day of riding tomorrow."

Ella laid down on a blanket and wrapped another one around her. The fire warmed her, even with the cool night air swirling through the cave. *Who could this woman be who claimed to be her mother? What's her relationship with Mr. Wyatt?* No matter the circumstances, it didn't excuse what he'd done to her. Her parents must've been devastated when they found out she went missing tonight. Everyone would be worried. Hadn't they been through enough? *God, I've tried to live my life for You. Why did you let this happen?*

Ella pretended to sleep as Mr. Wyatt's footsteps got louder.

Her heart raced as she considered him taking advantage of her. If a man would kidnap someone, she doubted he'd think twice about raping them too.

She heard him laying wood on the fire. The crackling intensified and Ella felt the back of her get hot. Her stomach clenched in dread as she tried to prepare herself for what he might do. She listened to every noise trying to imagine what it might be without looking. Finally, he settled down. Ella relaxed.

"Good night, Ella. I know you're not asleep. You must be scared and I don't blame you. I am a very light sleeper, so if you consider riding off in the middle of the night … don't. I'd hear you the moment you got up, riding alone in this country without a gun would be a death sentence. Be wise and stay here. You're tired, so get some sleep."

Before long, Ella's heart settled to a normal rhythm. It'd be foolish to take off, as she had no idea where they were. Clouds had covered the full moon, a storm might be coming in. She wouldn't be able to see her surroundings and she didn't have a gun. Her father had taught her survival skills, but now was not the time to put them to use. Her breathing deepened as she gave in to the beckoning call of sleep.

DARLIA SAWYER

Chapter Two

Shane smothered the campfire with dirt. Ella sat atop her horse, her hands tied to the saddle horn. The sun's rays were peeking over the tops of the distant hills, turning the sky a multitude of yellows and oranges. He glanced over at Ella as he mounted his horse. The early morning sun lit up her red hair causing it to look on fire. This woman was stunning with her dark brown eyes and face painted in freckles.

He had to be careful and not get involved with her. She despised him. If he could go back in time, he'd make different choices. Unfortunately, he couldn't undo what had been put in motion. Ella would hate him more when she found out who her mother was, but he couldn't dwell on it now. Shane had to keep them headed toward Colorado. If he didn't take her to her mother and get the money, a lot more people would be hurt. His eyes needed to be on saving the ones he loved, and not on this moment.

His parents would never forgive him if they learned what he'd gotten himself into. Although, his father wasn't the embodiment of morality either. He considered anything acceptable if it resulted in a win for his client. Shane grew up listening to his father's dishonesty and corruption outside the closed doors of his office. If his mother saw the true character of the man she married, Shane doubted they'd still be together. He provided an extravagant life for their family but at what cost? He used people to get there.

Shane could see now he'd followed in his father's footsteps and didn't even realize it. He wanted this to be the last job he would look back on with regret, it was time to be a better man. Once Ella was reunited with her mother, he'd move to California and start a different life. Far away from the ghosts haunting him in Cripple Creek.

"Are we going to sit here, or are we going to move sometime today?" Ella tossed her hair back and turned away from him, but he'd caught the fire in her brown eyes.

Shane moved the reins of her horse to his right hand and nudged his horse forward. He better watch his back.

~

Shane kept his distance from the more traveled areas as he didn't want to run into anyone but they were low on food and needed supplies. He bet most towns would've received a telegram to be on the lookout for a young red-haired woman who'd been kidnapped. He couldn't take Ella with him, she'd cause too much attention and if given the chance she'd be yelling for help.

He'd have to tie her up while he rode into town with the horses. It'd be a quick trip for supplies. They were halfway to Dallas, and he needed enough food to get them the rest of the way. It was growing dark, and the moon hid behind dense gray clouds. They'd have to stop soon because he didn't need one of the horses stepping in a gopher hole. He scanned the twilight and thought he saw a crevice in a distant rock formation that might provide shelter.

The last couple of nights they'd slept out in the open which made them targets, not only from wild animals but from outlaws who roamed the countryside. Shane could shoot with the best of them but he never wanted to be put in a life or death situation based on his marksmanship. As each day passed, he doubted the wisdom in accepting this job. He'd been very naïve to the ramifications of it, not to mention how much the hate in Ella's eyes seared his soul.

Over the last few days, Ella's intelligence had surprised him. Before he made this trip, he'd assumed she'd be an uneducated farmer's daughter. That assumption couldn't be farther from the truth, she challenged him on everything and did it well.

As they drew closer to the rock formation, it looked to be a good shelter. The crevice was deep enough to give them a roof over their heads, and they'd only be exposed to predators from one side. This also worked for keeping Ella hidden while he rode into town. The nearest town should only be a mile away.

"We'll stay here tonight. It beats where we've slept the last couple of nights." He untied Ella's hands and helped her off her horse. "If you get the blankets spread out, I'll build a fire." He watched her out of the corner of his eye as he gathered firewood. Why couldn't he keep his thoughts off of this woman? She brought grace to even the simplest of movements.

Coyotes howled in the distance. He'd need a large fire to keep them away, so he carried extra armloads of wood into the cave. There were two cans of beans and a few crackers left, barely enough to satisfy the hunger pains.

As he lighted the fire, he noticed Ella sitting with her head between her knees. She'd been quiet all day, not her usual argumentative self, trying to talk him out of taking her to Colorado. She must be resigning herself to not going back to, Nacogdoches. He squatted next to the flames and emptied the beans into a pan. Soon, the sauce from the beans started to sizzle, and he scooped them onto two plates and handed one to her. She ate in silence.

"Are you all right?"

"You're really asking me that?" Tears fell from her eyes and rolled down her cheeks. "I miss my family so much. I don't know if I'll ever see them again?" Sobs shook her body as she scowled at him.

Maybe he should've just let her be. She didn't want his sympathy. He'd tried to be perturbed with her, but he couldn't. She had every right to feel the way she did.

When she calmed, he ventured out to scrape off the dishes and wipe them off with a few leaves. When he walked back in, Ella had settled down and pulled the blankets up over her. From the steady rise and fall of her back, she appeared to be asleep. All the better, as there wouldn't be any further outbursts tonight. He'd get up early and figure out how to keep her from running away. He planned on sending a wire to Ella's birth mother while he was in town, letting her know they were on their way to Colorado.

~

The sun had been up a few hours when Shane rode into town. His first stop was the telegraph office. After that, he rode to the mercantile and purchased enough supplies for a few more days. He couldn't carry very much since they only had the two horses. The sheriff walked in as he finished.

Shane ducked into an aisle away from the counter.

"Good day, Fred. How's business?"

"Fair to middling. Was it a quiet night for you Sheriff?"

"Yeah, not much happening. I did receive a telegram this morning that said to be on the lookout for a man traveling with a red-haired woman. It stated she'd been kidnapped. You haven't seen any strangers fitting that description, have you?"

"Can't say I have, Sheriff. Been mostly men coming in this morning. I would've remembered seeing a redheaded woman."

"Well if you do, let me know. Have a good day, Fred."

Shane took a deep breath once the door closed behind the sheriff. Just as he expected, the word was out about Ella's disappearance. He carried his supplies to his horse and packed them in the saddlebags.

A woman across the street looked over at him and smiled. A hot breakfast at the hotel sounded good, but he couldn't risk it. Shane had been gone a couple of hours and had left Ella tied against a tree with her arms behind her. It had been weeks since he'd had more than beans to eat so the splurge on eggs and bacon would be a treat. He couldn't wait to fry them when he got back to camp. It might help Ella's mood too. Bacon could make anyone feel better.

Shane sensed an uneasiness as he mounted his horse, something didn't feel right in his gut. He kicked the horses into a trot. He had to get back to Ella as soon as possible.

Chapter Three

Ella opened her eyes. She had nodded off, waiting for Mr. Wyatt to come back. How many hours had he been gone? Her throat felt parched and she could barely swallow. At least the morning air was still cool. She laid her head against the tree, letting the breeze blow through her hair. She wondered how she must look and assumed it to be dreadful. Her stomach rumbled from hunger pangs as she thought about what kinds of food Shane might have bought.

A limb snapped and caused her to start. She turned her head toward the noise but didn't see anything.

Suddenly, a man came out from the bushes with his pistol drawn. "Well, look what we have here. A woman alone and tied to a tree. The perfect gift. How'd I get so lucky?"

Ella's eyes grew wide in fear, as she realized this man must be up to no good. His face had dirt smudges in every possible space. It was leathered from the sun and his evil grin exposed a rotting tooth.

"You sure are pretty. My boys will want to get a look at such a fine prize." He stood over Ella, staring down at her, unbuckling his gun belt. "But I'm not quite ready to share my good fortune with them yet."

He dropped his gun belt to the ground, pulled a knife from his boot, and cut the ropes, freeing Ella from the tree. He left her hands tied as he grabbed her under one arm and hauled her up against him. Her heart hammered so hard she knew it would burst from her chest as she screamed.

He slapped her across the face, knocking her head sideways. "This'll go much easier if you just cooperate and be quiet."

Tears sprang to Ella's eyes from the pain in her jaw. "Please, don't hurt me. The man who tied me to this tree will be back shortly, and he won't take kindly to you taking his property."

"I ain't scared of no one who's dumb enough to leave his woman unguarded. You should thank me for coming along, at least, if I decide to take you with me." He ran his fingers down the side of her face. "I might be improving your situation."

Ella turned her face away from his hand. "I'd rather stay here than leave with you."

He grasped her chin and twisted her face back to his. "That's not the polite way to show your gratitude to someone who's rescuing you. Seems like you need a lesson on thanking people, and I'm happy to be your teacher."

The man stunk so bad Ella gaged, she might

lose the contents in her stomach. The evil in his eyes penetrated her soul, causing her to shudder in fear. He looked at her like he wished to devour her.

He dragged her to where she'd been sleeping by the fire and flung her on the blankets.

"Leave me alone!" Ella shouted.

He tugged her closer to him as he knelt beside her. She kicked him but it did little to stop his intentions. She struggled to raise herself up, but he shoved her down so hard she hit her head on the ground.

"Stop!" Ella screamed at the top of her lungs.

The man slapped her again so hard she saw stars as he ripped the top of her dress open. "You need to shut your mouth."

Ella burst into sobs.

"Tears don't affect me. You, women, use them to get what you want only to turn around and treat us like dirt. I learned long ago women were only good for one thing."

A shot rang out, and blood spattered across Ella's dress as the man fell face first onto the blanket beside her.

Shane ran over, his gun drawn. He pushed the man over onto his back with his foot then checked for a pulse. The outlaw died instantly, a bullet through his head.

"Ella, are you ok? He didn't…"

Ella turned and looked at Mr. Wyatt, blood from the outlaw mixed with the tears on her face as she continued to cry. "No. Thank God, you got here when you did."

Shane gently helped her up and untied her

hands. He picked up his blanket and wiped her face off. He went to rub off the rest of the blood but thought better of it and handed the blanket to her. "I'm sorry, Ella, I shouldn't have left you here alone. I didn't know how else to get supplies without you causing trouble."

Ella's hurt turned to anger as she sought to cover herself.

"Risking my life is a better option than taking the chance I may tell someone you've kidnapped me? I'm of so little value, I'm worth less than a few cans of beans? I don't understand how you live with yourself after all the poor decisions you've made."

"Of course, I value your life, Ella. I value most people's lives except scum like the man who just tried to rape you. You don't understand. Other people depend on me collecting the money for taking you to your mother. I want to take you back home, I really do, but I can't. I couldn't risk you trying to run or yelling for help in town. It would put an end to any hope I have of paying those men back. You have to trust me. If you'll give me your word to go with me to Colorado and meet your mother, then I promise I'll escort you back to Texas. I'll let you send your family a wire telling them you're all right and will be home in a few weeks. I wouldn't ask you to do this if there wasn't so much at stake.

For a brief second, she had empathy for, Mr. Wyatt, but it quickly ended. This man had taken her from everybody and everything she held dear. She didn't want anyone to lose their life, but his choices had created this mess.

She didn't want to go to Colorado. Empathy for the woman who claimed to be her mother suddenly caught Ella by surprise. The notion she'd been taken from her mother never held any credence until this moment. Maybe the man who stole Ella dropped her off at the orphanage and said he was her father, not wanting to get charged with kidnapping. They had no way of knowing if he spoke the truth.

What if her mother had been searching for Ella her whole life? But, why would she send a private investigator to kidnap her? Why didn't she just come here and explain everything herself? Couldn't she travel? Mr. Wyatt hadn't said anything to make her think that.

"I don't know what to say, Mr. Wyatt. What have you done that put other people's lives in danger? If you had come to our ranch and spoke with my parents, I'm certain my father would have gone with us to Cripple Creek. He's good at calming tense situations. He would want to meet this woman who insists she's my mother."

"If I could go back in time, Ella, I would do that, but what's done is done. I've taken opportunities that were presented to me and wasted them. Made choices I shouldn't have, in order to make a name for myself. I needed to prove to my father I could do something with my life. He's repeatedly told me I'm a disappointment.

Instead of working hard to accomplish jobs the right way, I decided to take the easy road and become involved with the wrong kinds of people. I owe money from gambling debts. They want what I owe them and threatened to hurt anybody I care about. My family had nothing to do with my poor choices but may have to pay for my mistakes with their lives. Can you understand now why I kidnapped you? Your mother asked me to do this when I didn't have any other means to get that much money. It's my only chance."

Shane took a gulp from his canteen. "Ella, I'm asking you to help me keep my loved ones safe and for a few weeks of your time."

How could he put all of this on her? He made the wrong choices, but if she didn't help him get the money, it might torment her if anything did happen to his family.

"All right, I'll go. I promise I won't run away. We'll board the train to Colorado in Dallas. I'll meet this woman who claims to be my mother. You'll get the money you need to save your family. Then you can take me back to Texas or I'll wire my father to come for me. I hope this turns out the way you want it to, Mr. Wyatt. Shouldn't you tell your family and let them know there is a possibility someone might try to harm them?"

"There are reasons I can't do that. Let's get everything packed and leave. There may be men out there wondering where this man disappeared to."

~

The sun warmed Ella's skin as they traveled, helping her relax from the events of the morning. Ella had managed to tie and tuck her bodice to where it stayed up. Mr. Wyatt promised new clothes and a hotel room once they reached the next town. Their bedding had been ruined.

She never imagined having a day like today, where a man tried to rape her. If he'd taken her to the other outlaw gang members, they would have done whatever they wanted to her until they decided she no longer served a purpose. God had spared her from such a horrific ordeal but she didn't understand the reason for any of this. She'd been happy with her family.

Grandma Clara always said God worked all things out for our good. He took bad things and made them better. She hoped it to be true because what she might be heading toward didn't seem good. She had to rely on Mr. Wyatt keeping his word. A gambler was not someone you usually placed your trust in, in fact, it was a huge gamble.

DARLIA SAWYER

Chapter Four

Shane stood at the bottom of the hotel stairs waiting for Ella. He'd bought their tickets at the train depot. Their train would leave right about daybreak. Ella kept her word and didn't escape or alert anyone to her being kidnapped. Shane had left her upstairs to take a bath and change into the new clothes they'd purchased. After so many days on the trail, they desperately needed baths.

Bread baking aromas drifted from the dining room, filling the hotel lobby and making his mouth water. He'd been looking forward to a decent meal. When Ella finished getting ready, they planned on eating here, and he couldn't wait to savor every bite on his plate. It wouldn't be over until they'd eaten at least one dessert each.

He glanced up to see Ella descending the stairs in the blue dress they'd bought earlier. The dress hadn't looked near as good in the store as it did on her. It fit like it'd been made for her. Ella's red hair tumbled in loose curls down her back and her eyes lit up when she smiled. He couldn't take his eyes off her.

"Hi, uh, you look nice."

"I'm happy to be rid of all that trail dust."

Shane motioned for Ella to go ahead of him. "If the food tastes as good as is smells, it should be delicious. I can't wait to eat something besides beans."

Ella acted agreeably, but he sensed tension underneath the surface.

They were seated at a corner table toward the back of the dining room. The atmosphere was inviting and elegant but too dark. Only one candle had been lit on each table and one lantern flickered on each wall. The tables were covered with black tablecloths and the chairs upholstered in blue velvet. Other than Ella's dress, Shane had barely spent any of the money her mother had given him for travel expenses. They would eat well tonight.

"Order whatever you'd like, your mother gave us a generous allowance for the trip. I plan on ordering a sirloin steak with potatoes and gravy."

Ella placed a napkin over her lap. "I want the chicken and dumplings. I miss my mother's cooking. Chicken and dumplings are one of her specialties. A big piece of apple pie would be nice too."

"Apple pie. That sounds heavenly. My mother never cooked. We had a woman named, Martha, that my father brought in to cook. Her cinnamon rolls would melt in your mouth. We'll drop by my parents' home in Denver before heading to Cripple Creek. I haven't seen them in quite some time, and

I'm not certain when I'll be back."

Shane noticed Ella watching everybody who entered the dining room. Could she be hoping to see someone she knew? He wouldn't fault her if she had. It would be an end to this charade.

The server took their order and served them both a cup of vegetable soup. Shane had never much cared for vegetables, but tonight everything tasted wonderful. "I'm glad we're able to travel by train now. It'll make the trip faster and we won't have to worry about outlaws trailing us. You're anxious to go home and I don't have much time left to get the money I owe paid."

Ella stared at her plate. "Yes, I'm concerned about my family and what they're going through. I agreed to this because I don't want anybody to be hurt. I wonder if it was the right thing to do. My family's been through a lot the last seven years, and just when things had settled down, I go missing. I hope they believe the message I wired."

"I wish there was another way, Ella, but I'm out of options and time." Shane moved his soup bowl to the side as the server set his dinner in front of him. One bite of steak and he realized he'd made the perfect decision.

Ella took another sip of her soup. "I'm curious as to how you started gambling. You owe me an explanation."

"I don't want to talk about it, but you're right. My father wanted me to follow in his footsteps and become a lawyer. Quite honestly, many of the people he defended deserved to be in jail. He's good at what he does that's why they go free. My dream has always been to purchase land and livestock and be a rancher. He considered that an absurd idea, so I left.

Gold had been found in Cripple Creek, so I figured mining might provide a way for me to buy land. A month after I moved there, a fire burned half the town, and then a couple of days later another fire took all that had remained. It wondered if I'd stepped into the middle of a nightmare. They hired a lot of workers to rebuild Cripple Creek, so I kept busy and did well. They had the town up and running in a few months.

I met a couple of miners who'd staked a claim and were having decent luck finding gold but needed more help. They let me buy a share in their mine, and we did well for five months. During that time, I acquired a love of gambling. I had plenty of gold coming in, so I didn't worry about any loses. I put gold aside for the land I wanted to buy, the expenses I had and still had a generous amount left to gamble with. I made lots of money at gambling and became quite skilled at it.

But then the gold became harder to locate. As the mine dried up, so did my luck. I lost a lot of money and didn't have a way to earn more. Every night I told myself this would be the time I'd regain my losses, but I only lost more. I used the savings I'd set aside for the land. After it was gone, I started borrowing money and signing, IOU's. As you can guess, they weren't being paid back. I'd win a little cash here and there, but not enough to make a dent in the debt.

I met a woman around this time and we got

involved. She assumed I had lots of money because of what I spent at the gambling tables. I didn't tell her I was risking borrowed cash. Her father is Cripple Creek's doctor, and she had become accustomed to the finest of everything.

The men who loaned me credit weren't known for being merciful when you didn't make payments. At first, they gave me warnings because I still paid on the loan. As time went by and the debt increased they resorted to beating me. I feared for my life. I asked my friends for loans a couple of times, just to keep them from killing me. But the downward spiral continued. I lost my friends and had no means to come up with any cash. They cornered me in an alley one night and beat me up bad. They told me I had a month to come up with the money I owed or they'd kill everyone I love. My parents don't know about any of this, at least, not yet."

"That's quite the story, Mr. Wyatt. I've seen other men who've had gambling problems. Some managed to quit and their lives got much better, some didn't. I'm concerned I'll do this for you, then you'll turn around and make the same mistakes again. I'll have lost weeks of my life and upset my parents for nothing. I don't think you should stay in Cripple Creek after you pay off your loans. The men you gambled with are still there and they'll try to draw you back in. What would keep you from joining another game of chance?"

"I've considered moving back to Denver. There are better jobs there for private investigators." Shane motioned the server over to order dessert. They both wanted apple pie.

"You haven't changed anything in your life yet. How did you get into detective work?"

The conversation fell silent as the server brought their pie, and they concentrated on eating every last bite.

"I worked for my father as a private investigator before I moved to Cripple Creek. That's how I learned so much about the clients he defended. It's something I'll do until I find another job. Who knows, I may continue with it."

The server came by to check on them, and Shane paid her. "We should call it a night and get some rest. We need to be at the train depot early."

Ella stood. "I hope you're telling me the truth."

Shane followed her up the stairs and waited while she unlocked her door. "I'm trusting you'll still be here in the morning."

"I gave you my word." Ella opened the door and glanced back at Shane. "I'm trusting you'll keep yours as well, Mr. Wyatt." Ella smiled as she went inside.

Shane had no choice but to trust she wouldn't escape. She could have left earlier while he waited for her to take a bath and get ready, but she didn't. His room was next to hers, so surely he'd hear Ella if she tried sneaking out. He unlocked his door, went in and laid down on the bed. Within minutes, he fell asleep.

~

Shane helped Ella up the steps and into the train. They would be on the way to Denver soon. Ella wore the blue dress she had on last night. She looked as lovely today as she had then. Shane's thoughts wandered to what it'd be like to hold her. He had to stop thinking about her. There wasn't a chance anything romantic would develop between them after what he'd done to mess up her life.

They sat close to the rear of their train car across from an older gentleman with gray hair. Shane picked up a newspaper left on his seat as he sat down and leaned back. Ella stared out the window next to him He watched her out of the corner of his eye. She was the perfect mixture of beauty and intelligence. The train lurched forward, they were on their way.

The couple in front of them were quite cozy. Maybe they had just gotten married. The man whispered into the woman's ear causing her to giggle. He brought her gloved hand to his lips and kissed it. Shane raised his newspaper to block the view.

Ella stirred beside him and glanced over at him. "The last time I rode a train, I was an orphan on my way to Texas. I was so scared when we left New York City. I was older than most of the children and had no idea if a family would choose me. I'd cry myself to sleep every night not knowing what would happen."

Shane looked at her. Her brown eyes were shiny with unshed tears. "I can't imagine how terrible that had to be for you, Ella. I'm sorry trains don't hold very good memories."

"It's been seven years but seems like yesterday. If it hadn't been for my mother, Anna, who was our orphan train agent, keeping me, I would have gone back to the orphanage in New York. My dream of a life with my own family would've been just that, a dream. When my mother married my father, Joshua Brown, they made me a part of their family. They loved and treated me the same as their other children." Ella wiped a tear from her eye.

"Then I came along and took you away from everyone. I'm sorry. What you're doing for me is way more than I had a right to ask. The woman who hired me expressed she never wanted to give you up. I don't know the whole story, but she obviously considered it important to see with you. Not many people would go to such lengths and expense to find a child they hadn't seen in almost twenty years, knowing their now adult daughter probably despised them. I hope this trip will add something more than sorrow to your life." Shane found it tough not to gawk at her.

"This story is not what you'd expect from a woman who had her child taken. Why did it take her seventeen years to search for me? You would've thought she'd have tried before now. After I meet with her, I want to be on the next train to Texas. I have someone special in my life who has to be worried about me. I've been waiting for him to ask me to marry him. Our fathers are good friends, as they both own ranches, although Clint's father raises horses and my father raises cattle." Ella's eyes lit up and pink graced her freckled cheeks as she spoke about him.

Shane's heart sank. Of course, she'd have someone in her life. Why had he not considered the possibility? Maybe because he'd been smitten from the beginning.

"Did you hear my question?"

"Oh, sorry, I was thinking of something else and drifted a bit. What did you ask?"

"I asked why this woman would wait seventeen years to look for me." Ella glanced out the window again.

Shane assumed he'd upset her by not listening. "When you spoke of raising horses, I remembered as a child how much I'd loved learning to ride. My father has a ranch of his own outside of Denver, where they breed and raise quarter horses. He has a staff to manage it and tries to find time to get out there when he can. He wants to retire in the next few years and live there. I didn't mean to be rude, my thoughts just flew back to better times. But, to answer your question, she never said."

"Does your girlfriend know about the threats on her life?" Ella drew a hankie from her bag and wiped her forehead. "It's rather warm in here."

Ella's questions were causing beads of sweat on Shane's brow. "She was the first person they threatened to harm."

"Have you told her the extent of your gambling problem, yet?"

"No. She went with me sometimes so she knew I gambled but I lied to her about the injuries I suffered. One time, I told her I'd had a good night gambling but got beaten and robbed of my winnings on the way home. Another night, I explained some men were abusing a woman, and I got in a fight while struggling to stop them. I didn't want

Catherine to be upset, and I also wanted to spare myself from telling her the truth. If she found out, we wouldn't be together."

Ella looked at Shane with wrinkled brows. "No! By not telling her the facts you've endangered her life. How selfish of you to not understand that?"

The couple in the seat in front of them were kissing each other passionately now. It was awkward to observe them with Ella beside him. Shane wondered if they should change seats. This train ride would to be a long one.

Shane squirmed in his seat rehashing their conversation in his head. He envisioned Ella thinking how bad a person he'd been. After all, a guy who doesn't choose the protection of those he loves over his own personal pleasures isn't much of a man. She made it clear early on how she felt about men who gambled. There's no way he'd ever be more than a flawed man in her eyes. He turned his face toward the aisle. The silence felt deafening. Minutes seemed like hours.

"I'm sorry, I shouldn't have been so harsh."

Shane couldn't believe she'd apologized.

"No, I deserved it. I've put people in danger and made decisions because of my lack of self-control. I've endangered your life and put guilt on you in order to get you to help me. No one would consider me a good man."

"As long as you're breathing, there's time to change, Mr. Wyatt. We can right our wrongs and prove to those we love how much we've learned from our mistakes. One of the men on our ranch rode with outlaws thinking he didn't have any other choice. This decision almost led to the death of not only him but also another man who works for my father. Yet, Wesley has completely changed his life and proven himself trustworthy. He has a beautiful wife who's a doctor, and they have a delightful little boy. He's one of my father's best foremen." Ella touched his arm. "I'm giving you the chance to start over by going with you to Cripple Creek. I hope you honor my sacrifice. You can do better with your life."

Goosebumps from her touch ran up his arm and down his back.

"Thank you, Ella. I promise you I won't squander this chance. I don't ever want to be in this place again."

DARLIA SAWYER

Chapter Five

The brakes on the train squealed as it came to an abrupt stop. Ella braced herself on the back of the bench in front of her. Shane pulled his gun from its holster. She recalled, Dr. Sophie Johnson's story, of her train being robbed by outlaws on her way to Nacogdoches. She saved the life of her future husband, Wesley, after he'd been shot. She didn't realize the outlaw she dug the bullet out of would one day steal her heart. Ella hoped this wasn't a train robbery.

Her palms were sweaty and her chest tightened from holding her breath in dread of what might await them. They waited to hear why the train stopped. Shane sat on the edge of his seat. No one said a word, even the children were absolutely silent, sitting still in their seats. It was as if everyone had been suspended in time. Ella feared the worst but hoped for the best.

A gentleman in a railroad uniform burst through

the doors into their car. "Don't panic. There's something or someone on the tracks ahead. We need to investigate, so if there is anybody who will help, I'll take you to the man in charge."

Shane stood along with three other men. "I'll be back as soon as we find out what's wrong. It's probably nothing to worry about, so try to relax. Hopefully, it won't take long." He followed the other guys out the car doors.

Ella leaned back in her seat, and stared out the window, taking deep breaths to calm herself. It was overcast, and the skies were dark and threatening rain. The trees swayed from the wind of an impending storm.

The couple in front of her were whispering to each other. Their constant acts of affection since they'd boarded the train yesterday morning had finally come to a stop. Ella overheard a passenger with small children suggest they get a private car. They ignored the suggestion.

Everyone guessed what might be blocking the tracks. Some of the speculations were not good and Ella didn't want to entertain those fears. They had to be near the Texas border or in the Oklahoma Territories. If they got moving soon, they should reach Denver by tomorrow afternoon. They planned to stay the night with Mr. Wyatt's parents, then head to Cripple Creek the following day. Thoughts of meeting the woman who claimed to be her mother filled Ella with dread. She suspected nothing good would come from this.

Her mind drifted back to the last time she'd been with Clint. They'd spent the day riding across his father's property with his sister, Claire, who chaperoned them. Ella had made a picnic lunch and they stopped near a small lake. Clint talked of where he wanted to build a home. His father had given him a hundred acres and a few horses to establish his own ranch. He asked Ella how big she wanted her house to be. She'd hoped it wouldn't be long until Clint asked for her hand in marriage. He planned on building his home over the summer with help from his friends and family.

They'd been unofficially courting the year before she turned nineteen, the age her parents said she could officially court. The extra year gave her time to decide what she wanted to do and not rush into a relationship with anybody. She hadn't appreciated their decision then, but now she recognized the wisdom in sorting through what was important to her.

Ella enjoyed working with her town's veterinarian, Dr. Andrews. She loved helping sick animals. She'd considered going to school to become a veterinarian but didn't want to leave Nacogdoches. Ella never understood why people looked down on a woman doing other jobs besides being a wife and mother. She was thankful her mother and Doctor Sophie taught her it didn't have to be that way. Dr. Andrews wished to retire soon, and Ella wanted to take over for him. She'd accompanied him on house calls and he'd been teaching her everything he knew.

Suddenly, a deafening clap of thunder rang out, causing her to jump, and startling many of the other passengers. Its rumble through the train cars warning of the closeness of the approaching storm.

A man across from her stood and looked out the window. "This storm looks bad. The wind is really blowing."

Ella got up to stretch her legs and calm her worry. The train car rocked from the high winds. She spotted a small girl sitting alone a few rows up. She looked ready to cry. She squatted next to her in hopes of calming her fears. The little girl turned her face away from her.

"Hello, my name is Ella. I noticed you sitting by yourself and since I'm alone too, I decided to come say hi. Are you all right? Where's your mother?"

The little girl turned back toward Ella and pushed her brown curls away from her face. "My mother's dead so is my father. The woman I'm with went to the restroom."

"What's your name?"

"Susie."

"How old are you, Susie?"

"I'm eight."

"Is the woman you're traveling with family?"

Susie lowered her head. "No, she works for the orphanage and brought me out west to find me a family. No one wants me, though." Tears welled in her eyes. "So, we're headed back to New York City."

Ella touched the girl's hand. "Oh Susie, I'm so sorry. I was an orphan too and came out west on an orphan train. And, just like you, no one chose me either." Ella sat beside her.

"What happened to you?" Susie glanced at her with the bluest eyes Ella had ever seen.

"The woman who took me out here loved me and adopted me. She married a cattle rancher, and I found the family I'd always dreamed of. Are you certain there aren't any more stops for you to make?" Ella patted Susie's hand.

"No ma'am, we're going to Denver to get on a train back to the orphanage in New York City." Tears spilled from her sad eyes.

Ella's heart broke. How could anyone not want this little girl? It brought back the emotions of rejection she'd experienced as an orphan. She wanted to take her home to Texas. Her mother had established an orphanage on their ranch. They generally had around fifteen to twenty children there. Ella helped with the children whenever she had time, and they all loved her. Susie would be better off there than going to an overcrowded orphanage in New York. She needed to talk to Susie's agent.

Shouting erupted outside and Ella looked out the window to see what the excitement might be about. Another man burst through the doors, with a distressed look on his face.

"We have a dangerous situation outside. The train stopped due to an Indian tribe sitting on the tracks. At first, we assumed it was a ploy to rob us, but their chief was very sick and in a lot of pain. They stopped the train hoping a doctor might be on board. We located one in a forward car who treated him, but we have a more pressing problem arising. A tornado has formed to the west of our train, and it's headed right at us. Judging from the size of this tornado, we don't think it's safe to stay in the train.

There is a dried-up creek bed running along the east side of the tracks which could be your best chance for shelter. If the tornado continues on its path, it will go right over us. Please leave the train and run toward that area as quickly as possible. We're asking the men to help the women and children get there."

Everyone exited their seats and pushed each other down the aisle.

Ella grabbed Susie's hand. "Come on, we need to leave now."

"We can't leave, Miss Wheeler isn't here." Susie pulled back.

"I'm certain she's already on her way to the creek bed. We have to leave Susie, there's no time to wait."

A man paused to let Ella and Susie into the aisle in front of him. She pulled the little girl along with her through the doors, and down the steps. Ella gasped as she turned and looked at the western sky. She'd been through a few tornados living in Texas but only one had swept over their ranch, most had been a few miles away. This was the biggest tornado she had ever encountered. They needed to run. Shane ran toward them and took Susie's other hand. Small tree limbs and other debris flew through the air as they raced to the creek bed. Other passengers scrambled to escape. Some took their chances under the train.

A large group of people were huddled together when they reached the creek bed.

Shane looked to the right as he grabbed Ella's arm and tugged. "Let's move down there, the creek bed looks deeper." They ran about fifty yards, and he jumped into the creek bed, then lifted Ella and Susie down with him. They laid on their stomachs with their hands covering their heads.

The turbulence from the tornado filled the air with a deafening roar that was growing even louder as it came closer. Marble sized hail was blowing amidst the debris colliding with anything and everything around them. Thankfully they were mostly protected by the walls of the creek bed that overhung where they laid. Ella's heartbeat echoed through every vein in her body. She hoped everyone had found their way to the creek, as anyone left behind in the storm might not survive. She heard Susie crying beside her and drew her partially under her. Shane scooted over and laid his arm over them.

The pull of the swirling winds overhead caused Ella to fear they'd all be sucked up into the tornado. She heard what she assumed were faint screams and wondered if a few of the passengers already had been. The ground shook when one of the train cars plunged into the creek bed a short distance away from them. Pieces of the car were torn from it as they flew upwards in a spiral.

Ella cried out to heaven. "Jesus! Please protect us!"

Susie trembled underneath her but didn't utter a sound. Just when Ella thought they wouldn't make it, the wind calmed considerably. In fact, it ceased. The roaring sounds from a few minutes ago were replaced with an eerie silence, except for the ringing in her ears.

They laid there for a few seconds, ensuring the

worst was over.

"Jesus, protected us as you prayed," Susie said as she squeezed Ella's hand.

Ella smiled. "He did, didn't He?"

Shane rose to his knees and looked around. Light filtered through the holes in the clouds.

"Not much left out there. I don't think you'll want to let Susie look around. Not everybody was as lucky as us." The expression on Shane's face looked grim.

Ella shuddered. "I can help with anyone who's injured. I helped Dr. Sophie on our ranch and assisted our town veterinarian, Dr. Andrews. But, if we can't find Susie's agent, Miss Wheeler, I won't leave her alone. We don't even know what she looks like."

"You stay here with Susie while I go assess the situation. Maybe I can find someone who would volunteer to watch her, if I can't locate Miss Wheeler. I'll let you know if I find anyone."

~

Shane returned visibly upset. "I've counted seventeen dead, and there are a number of more missing. There are many injured, mostly with cuts and gashes from flying debris but others have broken bones and head injuries.

Luckily the only doctor on board, Dr. Clark, who'd attended to the Indian chief, survived the storm. After the doctor treated the chief and gave him medicine, they rode off on their horses at the first sighting of the tornado.

I informed Dr. Clark of your medical experience, and he asked that you assist him immediately. I haven't been able to find Susie's agent. I did meet a woman with a couple of little girls around her age and she's volunteered to care for Susie while you help the doctor.

Ella spent the next few hours helping the doctor treat the injured passengers, while Shane and some men started clearing the track of debris. Among the seventeen dead was Miss Wheeler, identified by the train conductor, who remembered her because she was pretty. He'd struck up a conversation with her and Susie when checking their tickets and Miss Wheeler had introduced herself to him.

Thankfully, the locomotive remained on the tracks as well as two other train cars. The remaining four cars were blown off the tracks, scattered and in pieces, including the one in the creek. It had killed several people. Ella realized they'd be dead if Shane hadn't decided to move them to a deeper part of the creek.

The engineer had stayed in the locomotive and survived the tornado. He believed once the track was free of wreckage he could back the train up and recouple the two remaining cars. They needed to place the bodies of the dead in one car, while everyone rode in the other.

It'd be dark in less than an hour, so Shane and the other men started moving the bodies. Better to get them in the car now, than waiting till morning. They'd finish clearing the tracks at first light.

The destroyed train cars provided wood for the women and children to build a large fire. They salvaged food from the dining car that was lying on its side next to the tracks, and many of the passengers were able to locate at least a few of their belongings.

Everybody's clothes were damp from the hail and rain, and it might get chilly during the night. They rounded up as many blankets and coats as they could, but they'd need the fire's warmth.

Stars twinkled overhead as dusk faded to night. Ella was astonished at how clear the sky became after the tornado. It looked like the deadly funnel cloud had pulled in the surrounding storm clouds and tucked them inside. So much destruction in such a short time. It had been life-changing and life taking. The mood was somber around the fire as people struggled with either how lucky they were to survive or how unlucky they'd been in losing a loved one

Ella glanced at Susie and hugged her. "I'm so glad you're fine, honey."

Susie hugged her back. "What will happen to me now?"

"If it's all right with you, Susie, I want to take you to Texas with me. Mr. Wyatt and I have to go to Denver, and then to Cripple Creek for a few weeks. We hope you can stay in Denver with Mr. Wyatt's sister, while we are gone. When I'm finished there, I'll pick you up. I will wire the orphanage so they know what happened to Miss Wheeler and if they are all right with my plans.

Once we're in Texas, you'll stay with me or we'll find a loving family for you. If you want to go back to the orphanage, I can arrange that too."

A tear fell down Susie's cheek. "I don't want to go back to the orphanage. I would rather stay with you."

Ella hugged her again. "You don't have to if that's your decision. I want to make certain you're taken care of. Whether you remain with me or not, I'll do my best to give you a family. Let's eat some food, it looks like everyone's in line. They only offered us one blanket so we'll have to share and keep each other warm. We should be on our way in the morning after the men finish clearing the tracks."

Susie held Ella's hand. Shane got in line beside them. They'd found plates and bowls and a few utensils lying around the dining car, but not enough for everyone, so they'd share the spoon they were given. Canned beans and meat were what they'd found the most of, at least, they wouldn't go hungry. They took their food and sat near the fire.

Shane glanced at Ella and sighed. "What a day. I never imagined anything like this would ever happen. We were sure lucky that dried-up creek was not far from the tracks, providing shelter to withstand the tornado. If we hadn't been near it, I doubt many would've lived."

"I don't believe it was luck. God protected us."

Shane picked up a small piece of meat with his fingers and ate it. "I haven't had much reason to believe in God. He's never been there for me."

"Mr. Wyatt, if you hadn't noticed another spot for us in the creek bed, we most likely would be dead without you making that last second decision. Then at the peak of the tornado, I shouted out to

God to save us, and he calmed the storm."

Shane sat still for a few seconds. "I don't understand it, but it does give me a reason to acknowledge there may be more at play here than I'd given much thought to before. I've always believed we make choices and those choices have consequences, and sometimes other people's choices have consequences on our life as well. Everything else is chance."

Susie interrupted. "Mr. Wyatt, do you think there are any wild animals out here?"

"If there are I don't expect any of them would seek to get close to us with this enormous fire blazing? The one thing we do have is an abundance of wood, and quite a few of the men have guns. We should be fine for the night."

"I hope so." Susie shivered.

"I'll be right here by the two of you and I have a gun," Shane added more planks onto the blazing fire.

They finished eating and Ella picked the dishes up. "I'm going to wash them with the water they have over there. We should try to sleep when I return. It's been a long, hard day." She left Susie with Shane. Ella cleaned the dishes and stacked them with the other bowls and plates.

After washing the dishes, a woman bumped into her as she spun around to leave. "So sorry, dear. I didn't see you."

"It's all right, I'm fine."

"How's your family doing?" The stranger inquired.

"My brother and I are fine. We're taking care of

an orphan girl, the woman she traveled with didn't make it." Ella hated lying but didn't want people to assume Mr. Wyatt was her husband.

"How tragic. How's she doing? My husband and I are traveling to Denver to visit our daughter. I'm grateful we're both all right."

"She's holding up pretty well, considering. But other people aren't. It's excruciating to lose a loved one. I hope we all can get some sleep tonight. Take care." Ella made her way back to Shane and Susie. They were looking for stars in the sky.

"Can you find the Big Dipper?" Susie asked as Ella sat next to her.

"I expect I can. My father taught me all the star constellations when we'd walk around the ranch." Ella pointed toward a group of stars. "It's right there."

"You're right. What about the Little Dipper?" Shane smiled.

"You go up and to the right a bit from the far edge of the Big Dipper's pot to find the end of the Little Dippers handle. The stars aren't as bright but it's visible."

"You must have walked a lot with your father."

"We did. He made time for each of us. Susie, we should get under our blanket and see if we can sleep."

Susie laid down and Ella pulled the blanket over them. Susie snuggled against her and Ella felt tugging on her heartstrings. Susie would be easy to love.

Shane laid a few feet from them. Ella watched as he tossed and turned. He balled up a couple of coats he found and put his head on them. He'd courageously helped her and Susie through everything today but assisted countless other individuals as well. She'd observed the type of man he'd be if he gave up gambling.

Ella watched everyone settle in and gather their loved ones close. Within minutes, the popping noises from the fire were the only sounds heard. Susie filled the air with soft snores while Ella's eyes kept closing. She glanced over at Shane he laid on his side watching her.

"You were brave today. What you did to take care of the injured helped the doctor immensely. Not to mention how wonderful you've been with Susie. Thanks to you she isn't alone. You're an intelligent and compassionate woman, Ella."

"Thank you. You helped so many today too."

"Only what had to be done. Good night, Ella."

Ella turned on her back and studied the stars. She spotted the Big Dipper again. Life had changed so fast. Had God allowed her to be on this journey to be there for Susie? He knew her past could reach Susie's heart. It brought back the memories with her mother on the orphan train. It'd been one of the hardest times in her life.

When her mother and father told her they were getting married and adopting her, she'd never forgotten how happy it made her. Ella wanted to do the same for Susie. Her eyes grew heavy with sleep as she gave in to the peace only God brought in the midst of tragedy.

Chapter Six

The shrill of a train whistle shattered Shane's dreams of the red-haired woman lying a few feet from him. He sat up and glanced toward the locomotive. The first rays of daylight were peeking over the hills in the east. Hearing the whistle meant the engineer had stoked the firebox with coal and it had sufficient steam in the flues to blow it and power the train.

The engineer blew the whistle again and slowly backed toward a couple of men watching to ensure the locomotive coupled to the first of two surviving train cars. Shane got up and ran over to assist them.

After coupling the second car, more men joined them, and they cleared the remaining debris from the tracks. As the guys removed the wreckage, they got a closer look at the devastation the tornado left behind. They spoke about the size and strength of it, and how thankful they were to be alive. Daylight settled on the land and they'd soon be leaving.

Ella and Susie watched them finish. Shane told

them to get ready they'd be leaving shortly. The conductor questioned if they had enough room for everyone. The ride to Denver would be long and uncomfortable, so a few passengers might elect to stay in the depots along the way waiting for the next train. Only essential belongings would be taken and must fit in the rear car with the deceased. A couple of men stacked the items as tightly as possible.

The women and children squished in the first car, two or more per seat, while the men stood packed in the aisle way. Shane breathed a sigh of relief once the train started moving. He didn't have much time left to repay his loan. He needed to get back before they suspected he'd skipped town. He refused to be responsible for what they might do in that event.

The last couple of days had been beyond anything he'd encountered before. Shane had never seen a tornado, much less been in one. The destruction to the train and the lives lost had been unthinkable. When they'd covered the body of, Miss Wheeler, and helped carry her into the back car, the reality of it hit him. This woman had traveled out west and died seeking to bring happiness to orphaned children. Why had he been spared, and she had not? She devoted her life helping those who needed her. He'd devoted his life thinking of what benefited and made him happy, no matter the hurt to anybody else. Didn't she deserve to live more than he did?

Even now, Shane chose to keep secrets from Ella. If he confessed the whole truth, she'd never go with him. He hadn't considered the repercussions of what might take place when he captured her, only his need for the money. She filled far too many of his thoughts and dreams, now.

After settling his debts and returning Ella to Texas, he'd go somewhere no one recognized him. He needed a new opportunity, preferably away from mining towns filled with gambling houses.

He watched Ella interact with Susie as she perched on her lap. She held the little girl's hand as she whispered in her ear. Susie had been lucky Ella was on the train. No one related to the little girl's feelings better than her. Until now he'd never contemplated what growing up in an orphanage must be like. You might not even know who your family had been. Nothing is yours and everything is shared. They didn't experience love in the same manner a parent shows their own children. Loneliness and sorrow would be part of every day.

Shane grew up in one of the wealthiest families in Denver but they never spent enough time with their children. His parents had relied on a governess to take care of him and his sisters. His father worked well into the night investigating and preparing cases to defend in court, while his mother attended social functions.

Shane enjoyed working with the horses his father raised at their ranch outside of town. He had a way with them and they responded to his guidance and love. If his father had allowed him to run the ranch, Shane couldn't help but think his life would be in a better place. Instead, Mr. Wyatt, wanted Shane to continue his legacy of being a lawyer. Although, if he heard the truth of what Shane had done, he'd be content with him being a rancher.

In a few hours, they'd be in Denver. He needed to have a solid story to explain Ella and Susie's presence in his life. Shane's father usually saw through his lies, he'd had plenty of experience.

Ella's family had sought to shield her from the ugliness of life. She'd been raised in a loving Christian home since being adopted. Ella believed she'd accomplish everything she set her mind to. Her family even picked out her prospective husband. He wondered what secrets this rancher had. It helped him feel better imagining her perfect future fiancé to have a few weaknesses. One thing Shane expected, is her future husband demanding he hang for kidnapping her. When he took her back to Texas, Shane should leave as soon as he left her at the ranch.

He needed a credible story Ella would agree with before they arrived in Denver. Maybe he should reconsider staying with his parents. Any cracks in the tale and his father would be like a hound on the trail of a fox. Susie shouldn't accompany them to Cripple Creek, so he had to find someone who'd take care of her. He hoped one of his sisters volunteered.

Shane looked out the window. Not a storm cloud in the sky. His mind drifted back to the horror of the tornado. He never wished to encounter another one. Soon, the rocking of the train along with the warmth of the sun's rays caused his eyes to close. He wondered if he'd fall asleep standing up.

~

The brakes on the train squealed as it slowed to a stop. Everyone cheered. He couldn't wait for a bath and a hot meal. They'd made two stops since leaving the tornado site this morning. He'd stood for over nine hours. The last hour he spent imagining how wonderful sleeping in a comfortable bed would be.

The conductor opened the doors and Shane hurried off the train. The journey had been rough for everybody. News of the tornado and how many lost their lives had preceded them. The conductor had sent a telegram to Denver at one of their stops. There were undertakers waiting to remove the bodies from the rear car. Grieving family members cried as they met other family at the depot. This trip had forever changed their lives.

His heart felt the anguish expressed on each face. He had plenty to be thankful for. There were moments on this journey he'd wondered if they'd make it.

He waited for Ella and Susie to make their way out. It was the happiest he'd ever been to see Denver. White fluffy clouds floated in the sky. Even with evening descending the temperature was pleasant.

Susie tugged on his arm. "Mr. Wyatt, can we eat. I'm hungry. My rumbling tummy needs food."

Shane chuckled. "Yes, I'm hungry too. What sounds good to you?"

"Fried chicken, it's my favorite."

"Well, fried chicken it is. I know where to get the best chicken in Denver. We might even have pie for dessert. How does that sound?" Shane smiled at Susie.

"Do they have apple pie?"

Shane put his hand on Susie's head as he looked her in the eye. "They just might have apple pie. You must've read Miss Ella's mind, it's her favorite."

Ella laughed at Shane. "Am I invited?"

"I suppose we can make room for one more."

Shane led them to Martha's Restaurant. They smelled the fried chicken from a block away. After ordering, it didn't take long before they had plates full of chicken, mashed potatoes and gravy, green beans and dinner rolls with butter on the side.

Ella pulled off a piece of the crispy skin and popped it in her mouth. "I doubt I've ever loved chicken as much as I do now. It tastes so delicious."

Susie put a spoonful of potatoes and gravy in her mouth. "The chicken is good, but so are the potatoes!"

At the end of the meal, Shane ordered apple pie for everyone.

After Susie finished, she walked over to the piano in the corner of the room. Shane explained to Ella the story he'd come up with for them to share with his parents.

They'd pretend to be a couple. Their story would be, he'd met Ella six months ago when she'd been in Cripple Creek visiting her father's relatives. They had traveled to Texas to meet her parents and seek their permission to court. Shane wanted to close up his investigation business in Cripple Creek while Ella helped her cousin care for her sick aunt. They expected to be back in Denver in a few weeks.

Ella told Shane she didn't like lying. She'd agree only because of the gravity of his situation. They'd never spoke about their relationship but Ella assumed Susie thought they were a couple. Shane explained it might be the only way his family would agree to care for Susie. Ella doubted his parents wanted Shane to move to Texas, especially if his father still had aspirations of him becoming part of his law practice.

Shane didn't expect they'd care since he'd been living in Cripple Creek, anyway. Once he returned from taking her to Texas, he'd explain to them it didn't work out. He came home to Denver in hopes of running his father's horse ranch.

Shane sipped the coffee he'd ordered with his pie. "After I pay for dinner, we'll get a couple of hotel rooms, take baths and have a good night's sleep. In the morning, I'll give you and Susie money to shop for dresses. I'll go to my parent's house and explain who the two of you are and tell them what happened to us. They'll invite my sisters over so we can ask them about keeping Susie while we're in Cripple Creek."

"I agree, it will give us time to find nice dresses. If we showed up in these dirty clothes, they wouldn't let us in. They'll have time to talk with you about the news you'll be springing on them. My parents would expect to be told ahead of time if I brought someone to meet them. I'll get Susie so we can leave." Ella stood and walked toward the piano.

~

The carriage halted in front of a three-story stone mansion. Shane hopped down and helped Ella and Susie out. His father had sent him to pick them up. The butler waited at the front door to escort them in. They walked down a long hall into a sitting room where Shane's father and mother were waiting. He introduced Ella and Susie.

"I'm John Wyatt. It's nice to meet you, Miss Brown. Shane told us quite the story this afternoon. It would've been good to see you before you left for Texas but it doesn't matter now."

Ella guessed Shane's mother to be in her forties. Her dress looked to have been created at one of the finest fashion houses in Paris. Her dark-blonde hair was drawn up with a pearl comb, soft curls framed her face. Two younger women stood a few feet from her, each wearing equally beautiful dresses. Ella felt frumpy in comparison and wished she'd purchased a more expensive dress as Shane had suggested. She understood how he'd been trying to help her. He knew how the women in his family dressed. They hugged Shane and smiled at Ella and Susie.

Shane's mother stepped forward and took Ella's hand. "I'm Irene Wyatt. This must be Susie" She smiled at her. "You're very pretty."

Susie smiled back.

Mrs. Wyatt continued. "I expect you're hungry, our staff has prepared an excellent meal."

If the smells were any indication of what they'd be eating, they were in for a treat. Ella glanced at his sisters, who talked amongst themselves. "Thank you for your hospitality. This had to be a huge surprise. We decided it would be best for Shane to meet my family since I'd received a telegram informing me I should return home right away. I wish we'd had time to stop here before we left."

"Did you have a chaperone?" Mrs. Wyatt asked.

"Yes, one of my cousins accompanied us to Texas, as she hadn't seen my parents in some time. She didn't stay long because her mother got sick so she went home to help care for her." Ella hated telling these lies. Why did she agree to be placed in this position?

"I'm glad the two of you didn't travel alone. It wouldn't have been appropriate." Mrs. Wyatt glanced at her husband, John.

"Irene, there are many circumstances where a man and a woman may have to travel alone. If you're on a train, you're not really alone, anyway." Mr. Wyatt patted his wife's hand. "It's not like they rode on horseback and slept under the stars."

Shane choked on his water, Ella's face got hot. She glanced away, hoping to hide the blush she knew painted her cheeks pink. She guessed his parents would figure out the truth before the night drew to an end. Neither of them could hide the truth very well.

The butler walked in. "Excuse me, sir. There's a gentleman here to see, Master Shane. I didn't invite him in as I've never met this man before."

"Thank you for being careful."

Mr. Wyatt looked at his son. "Who knows you're here, Shane?"

"I don't have any idea, I'll go check." Shane quickly walked past his father and down the hall.

They heard the front door close behind him.

Mrs. Wyatt talked with her daughters as Susie pulled on Ella's hand. "My stomach hurts." She whispered.

Ella bent her head toward her. "Are you sick?"

"No, it's all tight. Can we go?"

Ella hugged her. "Not yet, sweetie, we're supposed to stay for dinner. You've been through so much. I'm sorry your stomach's upset. Maybe you'll feel better after we eat."

Ella took her hand and walked to the window. She hoped to see who Shane might be talking too. She saw the street in front of the home, but nothing else. The leaves were budding on the bare trees. They would be sporting their bright green cover any day. She loved spring. Everything had another chance to start over after the long cold days of winter.

Ella heard the front door open and close. They turned toward the hall awaiting Shane's return.

"Who was that, Shane?" Mrs. Wyatt asked as he came into the room.

"A business associate from Cripple Creek. He happened to be in Denver and wanted to give me the information he'd gathered on a missing person case. He planned on leaving it here, so I'd get it as soon as I arrived in town. Instead, he just told me.

Mr. Wyatt poured brandy into a few glasses. "What happens to those cases once you leave? I'd love you to come back to the law practice."

"I'll turn them over to a friend. The town grows more perilous by the month. I'm not certain what to do next but will keep your offer in mind. Thank you."

"I'm glad you're leaving there. Cripple Creek is not a place to reside for long." Mrs. Wyatt glanced at Ella. "What about living in Denver?"

Ella noticed Shane's hands shaking as he took the glass of brandy from his father. It hadn't been a business client at the door. It must've been one of the men he owed money to. Mr. Wyatt offered her a glass of brandy but she politely declined. She'd never tasted the stuff and didn't plan to now, although, it might relax her anxious heart. She prayed silently instead.

A servant announced dinner was ready. They followed his parents into the dining room. Shane pulled out Ella's chair for her, then helped Susie sit beside her.

"We forgot to introduce your sisters, Shane." Mrs. Wyatt glanced at her daughters. "Too many things going on." She pointed to the older looking of the two, she had dark-blonde hair like her mothers. "This is, Lena, she's twenty-three and engaged to a fine young gentleman, Cyrus Baker. He's the editor of our newspaper. This is our youngest daughter, Alice, she turned eighteen last month." Alice frowned at her mother. Her hair color the same midnight black as the men in her family. Both sisters had blue eyes and dainty features.

"Nice to meet you both." Ella smiled. "I have four siblings. Two sisters and two brothers. My father's first wife died in childbirth after they'd taken in two orphans the year before. My mother adopted me when she married my father, and they've had one child of their own. I doubt there will be any more. My mother opened an orphanage on our ranch because she wished to provide a place for children who had nowhere else to go. It makes such a difference in how they adapt to a different life."

Everyone sat in silence, not knowing how to respond to all her information.

Mrs. Wyatt patted her mouth with a cloth napkin, then set it beside her plate. "How charitable of your mother. So you were an orphan? Do you remember your birth parents?"

"No, I don't." Ella glanced at Shane. His head bent forward as he moved the food on his plate around.

Mr. Wyatt took a drink of water. "How dreadful for you. What kind of ranch do you live on in Texas?"

"It's a cattle ranch. My father owns one of the largest ranches in East Texas."

"Sounds like he's doing well for himself." Mr. Wyatt smiled at his wife.

"He is. Our ranch is becoming a small community. We have a doctor, post office, and a general store. Someday it may be its own town."

"How impressive! Your family has done well for themselves. Has the ranch been in his family for a while?" Mrs. Wyatt's demeanor changed dramatically for the better.

"It's been in his family for a few generations. My father's a hard worker and makes good decisions." Ella felt insulted at their questions. If they understood their son's lack of finances, they wouldn't be so arrogant.

Shane pushed his plate aside. "Perhaps we should change the subject. I'm sure Ella isn't enjoying being interrogated about her family's wealth."

"We apologize. We didn't mean anything by our questions. We wanted to know more about Ella's family. She's the first woman you've brought home to meet us." Mrs. Wyatt smiled at Susie. "Are you taking Susie with you to Texas, Ella?"

"I am. I want her to have a good family to live with." Ella put her arm around Susie and drew her close in a hug.

Mr. Wyatt pushed his chair back. "Have the two of you decided if you are going to live in Colorado or Texas if your relationship progresses?"

"We haven't. I'll accompany Ella to Texas after we settle everything in Cripple Creek. I might come home for a time until we decide what our future holds."

"Writing letters isn't the easiest way to maintain a relationship. You might work there until the two of you determine if you want to make a commitment." Mrs. Wyatt asked the servants to bring in dessert. "How long will you be in Cripple Creek?"

"A few weeks. I'm looking forward to getting out of there. You both were right, I should have never moved there."

"I'm glad you've come to your senses." Mrs. Wyatt smiled. "If Ella had anything to do with that decision, we are eternally grateful."

Shane cleared his throat. "Yes, she did. And speaking of how rough that town is, we were wondering if you'd let Susie stay here while we settle my affairs in Cripple Creek?"

"How fun it would be to have a little girl around. Your sisters can help. If everyone's finished their dessert, we should move to the sitting room. It's much more comfortable." Mr. Wyatt stood and pulled his wife's chair out.

The rest of the evening they spoke about what Shane might do in Denver if they chose to live there. Shane told his father he'd be interested in running their horse ranch. Mr. Wyatt didn't like the idea at first but warmed up to it as they talked. Lena agreed to watch Susie while they were in Cripple Creek. Both sisters spoke with her while Shane talked with his parents. Ella sat next to him trying to pay attention to both conversations.

"Should I have the carriage brought around, or were the three of you staying the night in our guest rooms?" Mr. Wyatt yawned. "It's past my bedtime."

"We planned on staying here, father if it's not an imposition. Ella and I will purchase tickets tomorrow so we can leave the next day. It gives us time to buy clothes and supplies since ours were lost in the tornado." Shane took a drink of coffee.

"We didn't even talk about the tornado tonight. I can't image how terrifying it had to be for all of you. We've had tornados in the far eastern plains of Colorado but never in Denver. Shane told us earlier there were around twenty people who lost their lives. I'm grateful you all were spared." Mrs. Wyatt stood. "I'll tell Beth to ready the rooms. Do any of you need clothes for the night? We can find something?"

"We purchased a couple of items after we arrived in Denver. We should be fine until tomorrow." Shane stood. "Is there anything I can help with?"

"Of course not, son. That's why we have the staff."

~

Ella watched the flames devour the logs in the fireplace. She hadn't been this warm since they got on the train in Dallas. She'd never seen a more beautiful home, it was a mansion. Susie chose to sleep in Lena's room, so she'd get used to her before Ella left.

The fluffy bedding looked so inviting, Ella wanted to get under the covers. Shane had whispered he needed to talk to her before she left the sitting room.

A soft tap on the door startled Ella. She cracked it open. Shane stood there, so she quickly let him in before anybody noticed.

"You shouldn't be here."

"It's important." Shane stood in front of the fireplace. "The fellow who came by earlier warned me I had five days before they made my family pay. He's been watching the house for my return. I informed him I'd have the money shortly after I returned to Cripple Creek, the day after tomorrow.

"Ella, the more I consider what I've done to your life, the more I'm willing to ask my father for the money and send you on the next train to Texas. I'll be honest about what I've done and hope he'll pay my loans. He might disinherit me afterward but I'd deserve it." Shane sat beside her. "We wouldn't even go to Cripple Creek."

Ella scooted toward the arm of the sofa, putting distance between them. "After you spent the night convincing your father how valuable you'd be managing the horse ranch, you want to give it all up by confessing your past? Thank you, for giving me the option to return to Texas, believe me, a big part of me would love to go back tomorrow. However, I told you I'd go to Cripple Creek so you can pay off the money you owe and start a better life. If it's as simple as you've said, we meet this woman, she pays you, you pay your loan, we leave, and you get your life together, it will be worth it."

Shane put his arm behind her. "If everyone does what they've stated, then it should work like that. But when you're dealing with unscrupulous men, you can never be certain. If I confess everything to my parents, they will lose all trust in me, but I don't want to put you through any more than I already have."

Ella wondered what had prompted this change of heart. Shane had been adamant at the outset that they had to go to Cripple Creek. Ella didn't know what to do. She preferred to leave for Texas, but she'd come this far, shouldn't she meet this woman who claimed to be her mother? Would she always wonder, if she didn't listen to her story?

"I appreciate your change of heart. Now, that I've come this far I'm not sure what to do. I want to make the best decision for all of us. Part of me thinks I should see the woman who claims she's my mother. She invested a lot of money into finding me and I don't want to go through life wondering if I'd missed an opportunity to find out why I'd been given up. She would also have information about my father." Ella glared at the flames in the hearth.

"I'll leave it up to you. Tell me in the morning so I have time to either talk with my father and buy tickets to Texas, or purchase tickets to Cripple Creek."

"I will." Ella glanced at Shane. She'd avoided looking at him because of his close proximity. The moment she looked into his eyes Shane leaned toward her. She should get up, but something had glued her to this spot. When had she become attracted to this man? He'd kidnapped her.

Shane touched her shoulder, then moved his other hand to her face. His thumb caressed her cheek. Time stood still while all thoughts of why this shouldn't be happening flew from her head. His lips brushed hers. Shock and excitement shot through every nerve of her body. She'd never been kissed. She had been waiting until she married.

Shane pulled her closer, and claimed her mouth, his kisses leaving her breathless. He opened his eyes and searched hers as if seeking something. She didn't withdraw. He kissed her again and this time Ella kissed him back. They were lost in feelings neither of them expected. Shane ran his hand through Ella's hair twisting the curls in his fingers. "You're a beautiful woman, Ella."

"What about Catherine?"

"I plan on ending it with her when we get to Cripple Creek. I've never felt anything like this with her. You make me need to be a better man, Ella. When I returned from town and found that man hurting you, I realized I'd do anything to protect you. I want to be a man you can respect, but I'm trapped in the circumstances I brought upon myself." Shane stared at the floor. "What about Clint?"

Ella waited for Shane to look up. "Clint and I have known each other since my parents married. He's been a big brother to me, but there's never been any affection between us. I didn't recognize what had been missing."

"Your parents will hate me, Ella. When we get to Cripple Creek and you see the man who used to be a part of all that ugliness, you'll hate me. I've not been someone you deserve." Shane paused. "I should leave. Forget this ever took place, Ella. You'll be better off. I'll put you on a train to Texas in the morning."

Ella waited for him to look at her. He turned toward her. His eyes shone with unshed tears. He did care. She tenderly kissed him. "I can't leave. My answer is yes, I'm going with you to face everything. You may not have been the best man before but you can be, and I believe in you. No one can know what will happen. Right now, I want you to kiss me." She didn't have to ask twice.

Chapter Seven

Shane helped Ella from the train. "Welcome to Cripple Creek."

Ella held onto his arm as they walked toward the train depot. "It's bigger than I imagined."

"Since the first gold strike, it's grown by leaps and bounds, over ten-thousand people now. This area used to be nothing but cow pastures before they struck it rich." Shane's stomach hurt. The biggest secret he'd kept through-out their journey would soon be revealed. Once Ella discovered his misrepresentation of the facts, she'd hate him. He should have put her on a train back to Texas. The kisses they'd shared last night had stopped him from doing it. Although, Shane realized he'd been delusional thinking this turned out any way other than bad.

"Where do we go first? I presume it's to meet the woman who hired you. The one claiming to be my mother."

"It would be best." The weight of the

information he'd kept from her almost made it impossible for him to put one foot in front of the other. There would be no turning back now.

"Do we need to take a carriage or is it close enough to walk?"

"We can walk, it's not far."

The wood sidewalks kept them off the muddy street, but every wagon passing by slung mud blobs their way. Shane walked closest to the road to shield Ella. He hoped they didn't run into anyone he knew. He'd had their baggage taken to one of the better hotels in town.

Beads of sweat broke out on his forehead. It felt warm for the first of May. Only a few patches of snow remained from the winter storms. They walked past a couple of salons and Shane pulled Ella closer to him.

"Isn't my mother wealthy? This doesn't look like a respectable part of town. Are we going in the right direction?"

"We are, it's not much farther."

A couple of men whistled and yelled vulgar words at Ella. Shane glared at them while reaching toward his gun holster. The name calling ceased. They strode by a few more buildings and Shane opened the door of a place he had frequented in the past.

Ella took in a deep breath.

He'd never seen a room decorated more lavishly. Emerald green upholstered chairs and sofas trimmed in gold provided seating. Dark green curtains covered the windows. Women sat on men's laps as they giggled and whispered in their ears.

One of the women sauntered over to them. "Where have you been, Mr. Wyatt? It's been much too long. You didn't need to bring your own woman here?"

"We need to see Miss Fletcher."

"You mean, Belle. I'll inform her you're here." She winked and blew a kiss at Shane as she sashayed through the open door.

Ella pinched his arm. He didn't want to look at her but he had no choice.

"This woman who hired you is a prostitute? How could you leave that out?" Her cheeks turned a deep shade of red.

"I'm sorry, Ella. I didn't know how to tell you. The longer I kept it a secret the more impossible it became to say the words. Anyway, Belle's not a prostitute, well, not anymore. She's…"

"You didn't run out on me, Mr. Wyatt. I wondered if I'd see you again." A tall woman in a low cut dress walked into the room. Everyone stopped chatting and stared at them. Her hair the exact color as her daughter's. Ella wouldn't be able to deny the resemblances in their features. Belle had wrinkles from the hard life she'd led, but there weren't many women in town who matched her beauty.

"This is your daughter, Miss Ella Murphey Brown, this is Miss Belle Fletcher. The proprietor of this establishment and the woman who hired me to bring you here." He glanced at Ella. The color had drained from her face. He worried she might swoon. "We should go to your office. This is a bit of a shock."

"Yes, follow me."

She led them toward the back of the house, up some stairs and through the door to her office. A massive wood desk filled the front of the room with chairs and a sofa positioned close by. The same greens and golds were through-out this room as in the lobby.

"Please, sit down. I'm sorry, Ella, I hired, Mr. Wyatt, to bring you here. You're not tied up, so the two of you must've come to an understanding." She opened a small safe behind her desk and counted out a considerable amount of cash. "Your payment, Mr. Wyatt. From what I've heard you might want to get this to Mr. Stableman right away. He isn't happy with you skipping town while owing him so much money. I'd like time to visit with, Ella, so come back in three hours. She should know by then if she wants anymore to do with you. It will give her a chance to digest the shock of what I do for a living."

Shane turned to Ella. "I'll be back after I get this taken care of. I'm certain you're furious with me. I hope you'll talk to me later."

"What alternative do I have?"

"I'm sorry." Shane left knowing he might never have the chance to make this right, add another item to his long list of bad decisions. Last night Ella trusted him and let him kiss her. She had forgiven and believed in him. Today, he'd betrayed every bit of faith Ella had put in him. His words meant nothing, and she'd think he played it this way to get her here. At the beginning those thoughts were true. She didn't realize the more he fell for her, the tougher it got to tell her, her mother was the madam of the largest brothel in Cripple Creek.

DARLIA SAWYER

Chapter Eight

"I can't imagine how you're feeling, Ella. I hired, Mr. Wyatt, to take you from a life where you were happy. I haven't seen you since you were two. You were such a good baby. You'll probably despise me by the time I finish my story. I've had a lifetime of poor decisions but not being with you and your father is my biggest one. Don't blame, Mr. Wyatt. I preyed on his vulnerability. I learned he owed a considerable sum of money to some ruthless men because they frequent my brothel. I guessed he'd do about anything to pay back the loan and protect his family." Miss Fletcher coughed.

"My parents came to America from Ireland after I turned fourteen. They found work right away, and we moved into a rundown apartment building in a rough neighborhood. The rest of their family stayed in Ireland and I was an only child. They caught typhoid fever and died three months after we arrived. The orphanages considered me too old to live there, they struggled to find room for even the little ones. I searched for work, but jobs were scarce. The landlord kicked me out at the end of the month. I slept on doorsteps with a thin quilt to wrap around me. My stomach gnawed from hunger as I only ate whatever scraps I could find.

A woman who had walked past me a few times stopped and asked if I had anywhere to go. When I informed her my parents had passed, she asked if I'd like to stay with her. Cold and hungry, of course, I agreed. She let me in a big building through the back door. I recall thinking she must be wealthy. She led me into the kitchen and cooked us a meal when I finished, she gave me more. After I ate until my stomach felt it couldn't hold anymore, she led me to a room where I slept. She didn't say much, and I feared she'd ask me to leave the next day.

When I woke up, a woman took me to where a bathtub full of warm water waited. I relaxed in it until the water grew cold and then went back to my room. A dress and undergarments had been left out on the bed. I pulled the dress over my head. It didn't fit the best, but I loved having something new. It had lots of lace and ruffles on it. I found the kitchen and discovered eight other women sitting around the table eating. The woman who'd brought me to the house walked in and said we needed to talk.

She took me into an office and described the type of business she ran. I'd spent the night in a brothel. The woman stated she wanted me to work for her. She'd pay for my room and board, and even a little more. She explained what she expected me to do, the images bombarded my mind, making me sick to my stomach. I shouldn't do those things. My mother and father would be so ashamed.

The woman said I owed her for the room, food and the clothing. I could leave if I paid for it all, if not she gave me two choices, work for her or go to jail. I didn't have any cash and feared once I went to jail I'd never get out. That night I sat in her parlor while men looked me up and down.

No one requested me, and I'd never been so grateful. The next evening, Madam Lily, that's what everybody called her, ordered the other girls to put more makeup on me. She said the fellows thought me too inexperienced. It worked. I'll never forget the first man who raped me. I was forced to let him do what he pleased. Each night I went through the same abuse. Some men hit me while others did even worse things. I hated it and wanted to run away, but I had nowhere to go and no money to get there.

After six years, a young man started coming in and requesting me. We fell in love and I left Madam Lily's to marry him. After a few months, I got pregnant. He had a good job, and for the first time since my parents died, I had hope. When you turned two, the factory where he worked closed. We were going to get kicked out of our apartment and were almost out of food. An old friend told me about a woman starting a brothel and I talked with her. I offered to help her run it if I didn't have to be with any men. I promised to make her lots of money. She agreed, and I worked there so you'd have food and a place to live. Your father said to quit but I wouldn't. We needed the cash. He never understood and told me to leave. I'm not sure when he left you at the orphanage, because I never heard from him again.

I decided to move to Colorado. Rumors spread about how much money could be made at brothels in the mining towns. Towns were popping up at every gold and silver strike. I wanted to be on my own, so I could make my own rules. It's been profitable, and as soon as I'd saved enough gold, I hired private detectives to find you. You've lived the rest of this story." Miss Fletcher rang a bell on her desk, and a woman carried in two cups of water. "Do you have any questions for me?"

"How do you know I am your daughter?"

"My investigators ended up at The Children's Aid Society. They read back through their records and found your father's name with a note saying he brought in a young girl, named Ella Murphey. It was you. Your trail stopped at Nacogdoches, Texas, in the care of orphan train agent, Miss Anna Wilson. As you can see, our resemblance is pretty obvious too."

"If your story is true, it's tragic and I'm sorry you lived through all of those horrible events. No one should have to go through such awful things." Ella stood and paced the floor. "Why would you continue doing something you detested after you made enough money you no longer needed too?"

"Once you're a part of this sordid life, you lose any value or worth. Everyone shuns you as if you have an infectious disease. Men are the only ones who spoke with me and only in the brothel. I borrowed money to build this building. I had to pay it off as fast as I could because I refused to be at the mercy of men who'd stop at nothing to take everything."

"If the investigators told you I had a good life, why would you have me kidnapped?"

"I needed to see you and explain why you'd been taken to an orphanage. My heart hasn't been whole since I left you. He's never contacted me. We're still married as neither of us ever ended the marriage. I've never let another man touch me. I realize in my profession no one would believe me but it's true. I never stopped loving him.

"What is my father's name?"

"His name is, Robert Murphey."

"If you're still married, why do you go by Fletcher?"

"It's my maiden name. I wanted to keep your father away from the scandal of who I am. He asked me to not go back into the brothels. He tried to get me out of this life, and it worked for a time. I planned on only doing it until he found a job. He couldn't forgive me for going back when he had taken me out of it. He said we'd find a way through the hard times together, but I didn't trust him. I hurt him. He apparently considered it better to put you in an orphanage than to let me raise you. I can't blame him.

I haven't been a nice woman. I've had to be tough to survive otherwise I would've been taken advantage of. Because of what I'd been through, I don't force my girls to stay. They remain because I look after them, provide them a place to live and pay them very well. It's rough out here, the guys who move west can be criminals seeking a clean break, but few ever change. They find gold quickly and spend it on the pleasures they enjoy. Since there are fewer women than men it isn't hard to understand why so much money can be made in what we do.

I've broken laws and paid to have a man murdered because he beat one of my girls to death. There's always someone willing to do your bidding for the right price. When news got around that I didn't put up with them hurting my girls, most of it stopped."

Someone tapped at the door.

"Who is it?"

A woman peeked her head inside. "Mr. Wyatt has returned. Shall I let him in?"

Ella noticed Miss Fletcher frown. "I hoped he'd be gone longer. Let him in."

Shane stepped into the room. "I paid off the debts, they seemed satisfied, and so everything's good now. I'll close my business, then escort Ella back to Texas, if she's still willing to go with me."

"I hope you'll wait a few days to return to Texas. We've spoken enough for today, Ella. You need to reflect on all that's been said. I hope we can talk further tomorrow. Let's meet someplace else, so you'll be more at ease. It'll give you time to come up with some questions."

"Yes, I feel overwhelmed and need to think about everything you've said. When you decide where and what time we should meet, please deliver a message to the Palace Hotel." Ella followed Shane down the stairs and outside.

After they'd walked a couple of blocks, Ella

exploded. "Why didn't you inform me that the woman who thinks she is my mother is the madam of a brothel? Never mind. You realized I wouldn't come. You're obviously no stranger to her brothel. Even naïve little Ella must have limits to her sympathy and trust and you must've decided these truths would've hit my limit."

"Wait, I wanted to confess to you, but didn't see how. I warned you of the ugliness of who I had been. Yes, I knew you wouldn't come if I told you the truth. When I looked at you for the first time I realized she had to be your mother. You look too much like her. I needed the money desperately, but also thought I'd be doing you a favor. A chance to meet the woman who gave birth to you."

"The only positive that's happened from this, is finding out my father's name. Although, I wonder what kind of person he is since he never came back for me. All these years I believed my mother was dead and my father too distraught to care for me or also dead. She had an awful time after her parents died. She was left without a home or food and forced to sell herself for necessities. My father took her out of that life but when he lost his work, she went back to it. I can't help but think they could've found a different way if she'd waited."

"Belle never told me her story, Ella. I imagine she thought it to be her only choice. She felt desperate. She didn't want her family to live on the streets or go hungry. It brought up all those old memories."

Ella stumbled over a raised board in the sidewalk. She needed to be alone. When they entered the hotel lobby, she walked toward the stairs.

"I'm here if you need to talk."

"I've done all the talking I want to."

Ella walked up the stairs and into her room. She flopped down on the bed, buried her face in the pillow and cried. She wanted to go back to Texas and pretend Miss Fletcher didn't exist. She needed her mother, Anna, to hug and assure her they'd get through this together.

Why had she let Shane kiss her? Ella would have to tell Clint and he'd never forgive her. What had happened to her life? No one would understand why she'd kissed the man who kidnapped her. Ella didn't even understand.

Chapter Nine

Shane knocked on Ella's door the next morning but she didn't answer. She hadn't come to dinner last night, so Shane met with Catherine and told her he'd be leaving Cripple Creek in a few days. She hadn't been upset. He guessed she'd moved on to someone more respectable with lots more money. He'd never mentioned his father's name, or she might have held on to him a little tighter.

He didn't know whether to wait around for Ella, or slide a note under her door and get moving on what he needed to do. He'd planned on closing his accounts today and cutting all ties to Cripple Creek. He wanted to be ready to leave when Ella decided to go. The sooner they left here the better.

He should've never brought Ella here. It broke her heart finding out what her mother did for a living. Shane heard her crying last night. He should have borrowed the money from his father, settled his debts and took her back to Texas.

He made his way down to the hotel lobby. The

aroma of bacon permeated the air. He decided to eat breakfast before getting busy. He was hungry and Ella might be down. Her stomach must be filling empty after missing dinner. What a mess he'd gotten them into.

Shane sat at a table in a secluded corner of the restaurant and ordered coffee. He'd drink a cup or two before ordering breakfast in case Ella showed up. The door to the restaurant opened and Catherine came in, holding the arm of a mysterious man. Shane had been correct in assuming she'd found another love interest, presumably one with a well-cushioned bank account. They chose a table near the entrance. Catherine loved everyone to look at her. The waitress served his coffee, so he leaned the chair back on two legs and enjoyed it.

Ella walked into the restaurant. She had on a fitted white dress that accented her small waist. Her loose red curls draped over her shoulders and Shane couldn't take his eyes off her, she was gorgeous. Ella spotted him in the corner. Catherine studied Ella as she walked past, then she made eye contact with Shane. He watched her face redden as she scowled at him. Catherine couldn't stand being outshone by someone, especially in beauty. He wanted to laugh but managed to pretend he hadn't noticed.

He rose and pulled Ella's chair out for her. He made certain to be the proper gentleman. "Good morning, Ella, you look lovely. Did you receive anything from your mother?" Shane sat back down. The waitress interrupted them to take their order.

"She had a message delivered to me concerning

when and where she wanted to meet. It's at a nearby park in an hour. I'm not positive I should go. She told me a lot yesterday, what else might there be?"

"I wouldn't have any idea. Do you need me to go with you?"

"No, I'll be fine. I'm not sure she would talk as freely if you were there."

"You're probably right. On the way to the park, I'll show you my office so you can find me. If you don't show up before I'm done, I'll go back to the park. Are you still angry at me?"

"Yes, but it won't help, I need to concentrate on getting through all of this."

The waitress served their food. They'd both ordered bacon, eggs, and pancakes.

Shane noticed Catherine and her friend getting cozy. She must be putting on a show for him, expecting him to care. He didn't.

Ella looked behind her to catch who Shane might be watching. "Is she someone you are acquainted with?"

"It's Catherine."

"The one you were involved with?"

"Yes. I spoke with her last night and explained I'd be leaving Cripple Creek."

"Well… she's certainly not too heartbroken." Ella took a sip of water.

"I must be easy to forget. Once the cash is gone, the passion wanes."

"Some people discover they were never in love, they were only in love with the notion, while others aren't trustworthy. Clint would say I'm in that group if he found out what went on between us."

Ella cut her pancakes into tiny pieces.

"Neither of us planned on that happening, Ella. It just did. I won't apologize because when I kissed you, it was perfect. If you cared anything for me, those feelings have vanished with all I've done. I've kidnapped you, put your life at risk, and lied to you. There are too many things to forgive. I am really sorry, Ella. If I could start over, I wouldn't take you from Texas, but then I'd never know you. The same broken man would be making the same mistakes. Never understanding what he could be if he changed. The kisses we shared would've never taken place and that might be the saddest of all."

"We didn't plan it, but I didn't stop it. If I loved Clint would I have kissed you? I don't think so. I've reflected on this a lot and realized I care for him as a brother, not somebody I would marry. I tell myself the only thing I should feel for you is contempt after all you've put me through, but I can't stay angry. I doubt my family will let you near me once I'm back in Texas. They might forgive you, but they won't support me being with a man who's been a kidnapper and a gambler.

This time in my life is way bigger than anything I can handle alone. I've been dropped into someone else's story, where there's no happy ending and the plot is more than the heroine can get through. The villain has grown into the hero, and the hero a distant dream. Not to mention, taking in a little girl. I have no choice but to trust you'll protect me and pray you'll do what's right."

"I'll face whatever consequences your parents need me to. Whether it's to go to jail, or leave and never speak to you again. But right now, we have to focus on one step at a time. You have to meet with your mother and resolve where you want this relationship to go, then we leave for Texas." Shane ate his last bite of eggs. "If you're finished, we should leave."

"I am. I fear what will be revealed today, I hope it's not worse than yesterday. She has a lot of secrets."

"Maybe I should be there, at least in the background. I need to make sure you're all right. Cleaning out the office can wait. I'll find a place to hide, you won't even notice I'm there."

"She'll have her guards watching over us. When we left yesterday, a couple of men stood by the doors keeping watch, so we'll be fine."

"All right, if you don't need me there, I'll be at my office."

When they departed the restaurant, Ella placed her hand on his arm as they strolled past Catherine and her boyfriend. Shane felt Catherine's stare burning a hole in his back, but the heat from Ella's touch burnt away any thoughts of his former girlfriend. All eyes were on them as they left, and they weren't watching him.

Chapter Ten

Ella waited under the shade of a giant cottonwood tree. The trunk easily reached five feet across. Children raced around her, laughing and playing tag. She missed her brothers and sisters. They'd become so close growing up. Her mother and father loved and treated them well.

A couple of birds squawked in tandem in the distance. She wondered when Miss Fletcher would come. Shane had walked with her to the park, then left to take care of his office. She hoped they'd wrap things up in a few more days. The majesty of the mountain range to the west of Cripple Creek had Ella wondering what it'd be like traveling through them.

"Hello, Ella, sorry I'm late." Miss Fletcher sat beside her.

Ella hadn't even noticed, Miss Fletcher arrived. She'd been too awe-struck gazing at the mountains. "That's fine, it allowed me time to enjoy the beauty that surrounds this town. It's a lovely day."

"I agree. Although, my day hasn't gone as planned. My life is changing far faster than I'd prepared for. I didn't mention something important to you yesterday, but I must today. There's no easy way to say this, Ella. I'm dying. It's part of the reason I had to get you here as quickly as possible or I would not have been alive. I found this out a few months ago. The doctors aren't sure why I'm so sick. I don't expect sympathy from you, as you barely know me, but I needed to tell you, I love you, Ella." Tears streamed down Miss Fletcher's cheeks as she continued.

"I've always loved you. From the first moment I held you in my arms, I'd never seen anyone so beautiful. I wish I could express how sorry I am to your father as well." She wiped the still flowing tears from her face.

Ella didn't know how to answer. Yesterday she met, Miss Fletcher who claimed to be her mother, now she's dying. "I'm sorry. It's terrible you had to hear those words. Did you see more than one doctor? Thank you for being honest, it helps me understand the urgency in bringing me here. I'd wondered why you didn't go to Nacogdoches, it would've been easier than having me kidnapped."

"You're right, but my doctors advised me it wouldn't be wise to travel. The pain I go through is intolerable at times. I wondered if I'd even make it to the park today, but I'm glad I did.

There are other events taking place in my business you need to be informed of. My brothel has been very successful of late and a couple of no-good men are trying to run me out of town and buy the brothel. They don't know I'm sick and they shouldn't. I've tried to find someone to purchase it from me but the word is out these men want it so no one else will touch it. They consider women property and therefore should do what they're told. I've talked to my girls and told them to take their money and move elsewhere. They should build a different life for themselves but many of them don't want to. They've never experienced what it's like to work for someone who cares less if some man beats them to death. I'm running out of time. I have to be swift in accomplishing this before they take everything from me. My wealth should go to you."

Tiny roses in Miss Fletcher's hair comb matched the bigger roses on her dress. Ella studied her face, the dark circles under her eyes, the wrinkles around her mouth and the lines on her forehead revealed the story of a woman who hadn't lived a peaceful life. Her beauty still captivated but Ella saw the fatigue of too many burdens. Ella was moved by her suffering, even though she didn't understand the choices she'd made.

"I can't accept your money. It's not proper. Isn't there someone else who you wish to leave it to?"

"I expected you might not approve of the manner in which I made this money. I did it for you, Ella. I wanted to leave you security, so you'd never worry about where you'd live or if you had food to eat. I needed to take care of you since I didn't when you were growing up. You can give some of it to help those in need, like the orphans your mother devotes her life to. You are a far better woman than I ever thought of being. You'll use the money to make a difference." Miss Fletcher looked away, struggling to hide more tears.

Ella noticed the men from the brothel yesterday were standing close by. "I'm not sure what to say. My heart grieves for all you've been through."

"Please, say yes. I chose to go back to a life I'd already given up. I made that decision at a time of desperation to be able to pay our rent and buy food. I doubted I'd ever be a good mother or wife. I didn't have enough determination to resist the fear and make the right choice to be who you and your father needed. This is my one redeeming act, Ella, don't deny me this opportunity."

"Are you positive there is nothing the doctors can do to help you? If you go back east, you may be able to locate someone who understands what's wrong. Doctor Sophie, who lives on our ranch, is always telling us how new diseases are being identified and the treatments for them."

"Thank you, Ella. I've been seen by well-known doctors back east. None of them offered any hope. Even if they figured out what's wrong, it's progressed beyond the stage they could treat me. Don't be sad. I'm tired of regretting my life and it's too late to change it. Life doesn't always let us do things over if we mess up the first time." Miss Fletcher fanned herself. "If I've learned anything, it's don't remain in a dangerous situation. Do everything you can to get out and stay out. It may look impossible, but the alternative will leave you filled with regret."

"I wish I remembered you. I grew up believing my mother died and my father either didn't want me or didn't have a way to support me. When I came out west on the orphan train, no one chose me in any of the towns we stopped at. I felt unlovable. Once Anna took me under her care, things changed. When she and Joshua informed me they wanted to adopt me, I realized I'd always be loved. It's never too late to be restored by a Savior who has always loved you and always will. He can transform your life in a minute and your past is forgiven."

"I'm beyond redemption. I'm thankful you found a family. I've said all I should today. Time for me to go back to the brothel, my stomach isn't doing well. I'll send another note when we can meet again." Miss Fletcher tried to stand but her knees buckled and one of her men caught her before she fell.

Ella's eyes get teary. "Do you need me to go with you?"

"No, my guards will make certain I get back. Showing any compassion for me, after all, I've done to your life, Ella is far beyond what I deserve. I'm not going to burden you with anything else." She turned and walked away, leaning heavily into one of the men.

Ella sat suspended in time. This had turned into a nightmare. She found her birth mother only to discover she's dying and being blackmailed by awful men. Ella wished her mother and father were here to help her figure this out.

She strode toward the main part of town. She had to send a telegram to them and tell them how much she loved them.

DARLIA SAWYER

Chapter Eleven

Knocking on the door woke Ella from a sound sleep. She glanced toward the window, only darkness greeted her.

"Who is it?" Ella asked.

"Matthew, from the front desk. A man delivered a note for you and said it's urgent."

"Can you slip it under the door?"

"Yes, Ma'am."

"Thank you." A white paper slid under her door. She swung her legs out of bed and tiptoed over the icy floor to grab the note and then jumped back in bed. A message delivered in the middle of the night can't be good. She opened it.

Ella,
Can you and Mr. Wyatt, come to the brothel. It's an emergency.
Please hurry,
Belle

Ella put her dress on and slipped her shoes on. She pulled her hair up and tapped on Shane's door. He answered after a few seconds, he'd put on his pants, but no shirt. Ella couldn't help gawking at his muscled chest and stomach. She wouldn't admit it, but the sight left her a little breathless.

"I assume you need something, otherwise you wouldn't be knocking on my door in the middle of the night." Shane grabbed his shirt off a chair.

"The hotel clerk brought this note to me." Ella handed Shane the paper from Belle.

Shane read it. "Well, let's go." He pulled his boots on and buttoned his shirt on the way down the stairs. "I forgot my coat. I hope it's not too cold outside. Don't you need some kind of wrap?"

"I'll be fine. It's not far. Sounds like we should get there right away."

The full moon lit the street as they hurriedly walked to the brothel. The chill seeped through Ella's thin dress, making her wish she'd grabbed the wrap. She shivered and glanced behind them. Something didn't feel right, so she picked up her pace. Shane looked unaffected to the strange sensations disturbing her.

When they pulled on the door to the brothel it opened and they were greeted with silence. How odd. Their steps echoed on the wood floor. One of the girls popped around the corner and Ella almost jumped into Shane's arms.

"Belle is in her office waiting for you." She whispered. "Follow me."

She led them to Belle's closed doors and knocked lightly.

"Come in."

Belle sat in front of a fireplace, but there was no fire in the hearth. A man stood near a corner absorbed by the shadows. He stared at them as they went in. Something must be terribly wrong.

"Thanks for coming, Ella, Mr. Wyatt. I wouldn't have summoned you here in the middle of the night if it hadn't been an emergency. I'm very concerned about what, Jim Janson and his partners might try next. All but two of my girls packed up and left tonight. He offered them twice what I had been paying them.

He told one of them to give me a message. If I don't sell the building to him, he'll get it eventually, no matter the cost. Janson could purchase his own property and build a brothel, but he wants to be the only bordello in town. He's shut the rest of them down. Since I won't accept the small amount he offered, he's determined to not stop until he takes it. At this point, even if I sold it to him he wouldn't quit until he drove me out of here, or worse. I won't tolerate a bully forcing me to give away everything I've worked so hard for. I plan on fighting him on his terms, and it might get ugly."

"How can you fight this and your illness? You should just sell it and move to Texas." Ella wondered why she'd suggested Texas.

"I've never backed down from a battle. Even though it may be my last, it doesn't mean I won't give it my all. I didn't want to tell you about this, but they figured out you're my daughter. One of the girls told them why I'd been talking with you. Janson threatened to take you for his wife or make you work for him."

"No one could force me to do that."

"You don't understand how evil these men are. There are no boundaries where they won't go. They only care about themselves and what they want, and it doesn't matter who they hurt or kill to get it."

"If you were married, and I bequeathed my property to you, it would be harder for them to take it away, than if you were a single woman. A man has more rights than a woman. That's why I've asked my friend, Judge Morgan, to be here. He's willing to marry the two of you tonight, then file the license first thing in the morning. I'm sorry, Ella, I should've never forced you to come here. I wanted a chance to meet you and explain all that happened in my life before I died, but I was only thinking about myself. You can have the marriage annulled once you get back to Texas."

"Wait, you want us to marry?" Shane moved from behind Ella to face Belle.

"It would be a marriage in name only. You wouldn't demand anything from Ella, and I'd pay you handsomely for keeping her safe and returning her to Texas when this is over." Belle wrapped a shawl tighter around her. "Would you mind getting a fire burning, Mr. Wyatt? I'm afraid with all that's happened tonight, I haven't gotten to it. We don't want the two of you freezing while you're saying your wedding vows. I'll have Rose heat water for tea." Belle rang for her.

"Of course, but no one said we agreed to get married. Wouldn't it be better if we just headed to Texas tomorrow?" Shane laid the wood in the hearth. It wasn't long before a roaring fire warmed the chilly room.

"I doubt they'd let you get far before they killed you or took the two of you hostage. If we fight them together, we'll be stronger. We have to be a step or two ahead of them if we plan on protecting ourselves and getting through this on top. We have to be prepared for anything." Belle sat up straight. Her hands stiffened on the arms of her chair.

Ella noticed them trembling. "Are you feeling all right?"

"I'm having some discomfort, but the doctor says it's normal. It hurts, but it's not unbearable." Rose brought in a teapot, cups, tea, and sugar cubes. "Thank you. Would you mind pouring? I'm not feeling up to the task at the moment." Belle closed her eyes. "We should get this ceremony underway.

You should stay here. There is a room downstairs that our cook resided in. You'll be the most comfortable there. Tomorrow you should have your belongings brought here. If we're all in the same place, it will help the guards keep track of everyone. I have connections with some tough men who owe me a favor. I plan on hiring them for protection. All my attention will be concentrated on keeping us safe while we win this battle."

Shane stepped back from the hearth. The room warmed quickly. "You want us to get married and stay here in the brothel?"

"Yes, it'll be best if we're together. You'll stay in the room with Ella. I don't want her left alone. We can move another bed in there."

Belle took a sip of her tea. "I realize you'd

prefer not to marry someone you aren't in love with, Ella. But again, it's a marriage in name only for your safety. I'll be talking to the sheriff tomorrow. He owes me and better not leave me alone dealing with these criminals. Why don't we get started?"

Judge Morgan looked at Shane and Ella. "Are the two of you in agreement?"

Ella glanced at Belle. "I don't know what to think or agree too. I find it hard to believe marrying Shane will keep me or anybody else safe. They can take me married or not."

"If something happens to me or this illness kills me and you inherit this property and my wealth, it will be better for you with a husband. I'd be the last one to suggest you need a man in your life. I've survived alone for the most part, but you don't understand the cruelty of these men. Mr. Wyatt has dealt with cold-blooded criminals like them, and he understands their brutality. It's a sensible decision, and as I mentioned, you can annul it later." Belle finished her tea.

Shane moved closer to Ella. "Belle knows about the politics and corruption in this town, and what she's saying makes sense. I'll marry you if it's what you want, Ella. I'll protect you with my life. I owe you that much for putting you in the midst of this."

"All right. I'm trusting your judgment on this, Belle because you've convinced me you're my birth mother and you want to protect me." Ella couldn't help think this moment would change her life forever.

"Let's get started." Judge Morgan said. "If you'll repeat these words after me, we'll have this done quickly." The judge led them through their wedding vows. When he pronounced them man and wife, Shane kissed her on the cheek.

"Thank you, Judge Morgan, for coming here in the middle of the night and performing this ceremony. You're welcome to stay in one of the rooms, rather than going back out this late. Mr. Wyatt, let's move another bed into the cook's former room. Maybe we can get a few hours of sleep before morning. I'll have Rose bring you a nightgown, Ella.

They went downstairs to the room they'd be sharing. It was as large as two normal sized rooms. Ella made the bed she'd be sleeping in while Shane moved in a smaller bed, then built a fire in their hearth. After everyone left, she sat on the edge of her bed and watched him.

"You should get ready for bed. It's going to be a short night. I'll stay turned around until you change and tell me you're done."

Ella quickly took off her dress and pulled a nightgown on. After slipping it over her head, she gasped when she realized how low cut it was. She got into bed and drew the blankets up to her chin. "Ok, you can turn around now."

"Looks like you got yourself covered up. It's only fair you turn your head now while I get undressed."

"Of course." Ella's cheeks grew warm. She turned toward the opposite wall.

"No peeking."

"I'm not. Why would I peek?"

"Cause you can't resist looking at me."

"Believe me, I can."

"Well, I'll admit I may have glanced over my shoulder once. That nightgown gives a lovely view of my wife's assets."

"You're awful." Ella threw a pillow at him.

"I've been called worse. God must be thinking favorably of me to drop such a beautiful wife into my life."

"It's just pretend."

"I expect the law might judge differently." Shane chuckled.

"You are insufferable." Ella laid down on the one pillow she had left.

"If you get cold in the midst of the night, you might be able to persuade me to keep you warm."

"I'd rather freeze."

"I'm trying to take your safety into consideration."

"I'm sure you are. As long as you keep the fire burning I'm positive it'll be warm enough." Ella turned over and shut her eyes.

"I realize this pretend marriage is for your protection and I'll abide by that. But, if you ever wish to make it a real marriage, let me know. I just might agree." Shane threw the pillow back at her.

"I'm still struggling to wrap my mind around the fact my birth mother is alive and the madam of a brothel, and I just married the man who kidnapped me. Just saying that causes me to wonder if I've gone crazy."

"You got caught up in the poor choices others made. You've been incredible through all of it, your strength amazes me." Shane got into his bed.

"I couldn't have survived this on my own without God's strength. Goodnight, Shane."

DARLIA SAWYER

Chapter Twelve

Shane opened his eyes to the sun shining through the window. Ella still slept, her red hair laid in waves over the pillow behind her. He gazed at her, wishing things were normal between them. He wouldn't allow himself to imagine how everything would be different if they were married for real. Mistakes wove like vines through Shane's life, wrapping themselves around his dreams and slowly strangling the hope underneath. He had to let this go. With the threat of violence against Belle and Ella a reality, he needed to stay sharp. There'd be no room for failure.

He stretched his arms over his head. The aroma of bacon tickled his nose, or it might be his armpits. Shane laughed at himself as he pulled on his pants, grabbed his shirt and quietly went out the door, closing it behind him. He hoped there would be coffee brewed in the kitchen. The woman who helped Belle last night stood at the stove cooking bacon, eggs, and pancakes.

"Good morning." Shane tried not to startle her,

but she still jumped. "Sorry, I didn't want to frighten you."

"It's fine. With all the threats lately, I'm on edge. Are you hungry?" She tossed her blonde hair over her shoulder. "Belle asked me to cook for everybody."

"I am. But, let me find out if Ella is awake yet." As he spoke, she came through the doorway.

"I'm awake. You woke me up when you closed the door. I realized I'd better get up since I don't know what time it is."

The woman carried a plate over to the table and sat it in front of Shane. "Sit down and I'll get your plate."

"Thank you. What's your name?" Ella pulled out a chair.

"My name's Rosemary, but everyone calls me, Rose."

"Beautiful name." Ella took a piece of bacon off Shane's plate. "How long have you lived here?"

"Five years. I've saved up a nice amount of money and plan on moving somewhere soon. I look forward to doing what I want to. Belle isn't your typical madam, we're free to leave when we want. She's paid us well. I've been able to save money so I can start a new life." She sat a plate of food in front of Ella.

"You couldn't have been very old, five years ago. You look like a teenager now." Ella took a bite of her pancake.

"Fifteen. My father kicked me out and informed me he wouldn't be supporting me anymore. He gave me enough money for a train ticket and said good luck. My mother died right after I turned seven, so I had no choice but to live with him. He only tolerated me so he'd have someone to clean his house and cook meals. I never looked back and will never go back." Rose fixed herself a plate of food and sat with them.

"How sad. Maybe he regrets his decision now. I'm sorry you had such an awful childhood. The pancakes are delicious." Ella got up. "Anyone else want coffee?"

"I'm sorry, I should have asked." Rose stood up.

"Don't worry about it. Enjoy your food. It's the least I can do after you made such an incredible breakfast." Ella brought them each a cup of coffee.

Shane tasted the dark liquid, strong, just how he liked it. "Guess that means I'm stuck with dishwashing duty."

"No, Belle said you needed to go to the hotel and pick up your things. She's also arranged a meeting for later this morning. I'll take care of the dishes. Not much else going on." Rose looked at her plate.

"Change is rough, but it usually brings good things." Ella finished eating. "We should get ready. I want to see if I've got a telegram waiting at the hotel."

~

Shane and Ella strolled into the hotel lobby. She went up to the front desk to see if a telegram had been delivered. The man handed her a piece of paper. Shane walked over and she let him read it.

Ella,

We're glad you're safe. Your father and I were so worried. Hearing a private investigator contacted you and you had to leave right away to be able to meet your birth mother explains your leaving a little better. We still have lots of questions and can't wait until you're back home. We love and miss you.

Shane smiled as he handed the paper back to Ella. "Thanks for letting them think the best of me for a while longer. Although, if they'd send the cavalry, it might tip the odds in our favor."

When they got to their rooms, both doors were slightly ajar.

Shane drew his pistol from the holster and stepped in front of Ella, as he opened the door all the way. "Let me go first." Ella's clothes were strewn everywhere. A note laid on top of her bed. "The room's clear, but whoever did this left this warning." Shane read it aloud. "Leave town and never return if you wish to stay alive." They went in Shane's room and discovered it to be much the same, only his paper said he'd be a dead man if he remained in town.

"Well, Belle isn't lying. We need to get you a gun. I assume you've shot one before?"

"Yes, I'm quite good. My father made certain of it."

"You may need to be. We're outnumbered unless Belle rounds up those gunslingers who owe her a favor."

Shane stopped by the front desk and informed the clerk their rooms had been ransacked. He said no one mentioned seeing anything out of the ordinary. Shane didn't believe him, he'd been paid off. They walked back to the brothel. Every person on the street looked sinister. He made sure to check out the proximity of their hands to their gun holsters.

When they stepped into the lobby of the brothel, Belle was speaking to a group of men. Shane sat their bags down. "Gentlemen, this is my daughter Ella, and her husband, Shane. Your number one job is to keep them safe. I'm paying you a lot of money, so I expect your bravery and loyalty. With your help, we will win this war. Ella and Shane are staying here. So, the sooner we get a strategy together the better.

As you are aware, my girls were offered twice what they make here, so all but two of them left. I realize who my friends are now. These criminals want my building and my business, and they've paid off many of the leaders in town to do whatever they want. They had a notice served to me saying I've been operating illegally and there were heavy fines added to it. They hope to crush me because I didn't accept their offer when they came to me. Anyone who dares to stand up to them is signing their death certificate. They want me dead or penniless, nothing else will satisfy them. They know Ella is my daughter, and that gives them more leverage. Even the sheriff informed me his hands are tied, and we're on our own. He encouraged me to leave."

Belle walked over to a chair and sat down. "I've never backed down from a confrontation and I'm not gonna start now. I won't let anyone take what I've worked my whole life for. Gentlemen, there are plenty of rooms and beds here for you. We don't know what their next move is, but we will be ready for anything. If you can't commit to staying with me until this is finished, you should walk away now. I need men who will stand for what's right, not be bought with a few more dollars."

No one moved.

Belle looked pale. Shane hoped the men didn't notice. If they realized they were fighting a battle for a dying woman, he doubted they'd remain.

"Are you all with me?" The men shook their heads in agreement.

"Good. Then let's get a game plan in place. It's better to be on offense than on defense."

They spent the rest of the afternoon forming their attack. They'd need luck and ingenuity to catch these guys off guard. Janson and his men were not acting in secret, and the town officials were doing nothing about it.

Shane glanced at Ella. She'd stayed quiet through the meeting. Fear had to be gnawing at her, not seeing a way out of this. He had a hard time keeping his own worries at bay. If anything happened to Ella, he'd never forgive himself.

Shattering glass fractured his thoughts. A rock crashed through the window.

Ella grabbed his arm. "There's something attached to that rock. It's another note."

Belle glanced at her. "There were other notes?"

"Yes, our hotel rooms had been ransacked when we got our things. They'd left notes saying if we didn't get out of town we'd be dead." Ella's eyes shone with unshed tears.

Belle stood and walked over to her. "Why didn't you tell me?"

A tear ran down Ella's cheeks. "I was waiting for the right moment."

"Honey, you can interrupt me at any point. All information is important. I'd put you and Shane on the next train if I thought you'd be safe, but it's not how they work. You're their enemy because of being my daughter. I should've left the past in the past. I never meant for any of this to happen." Belle hugged her.

Ella rested in her hug for a second, as tears fell down her cheeks, and then she backed away. "It's been too much."

"I understand, honey." Belle went back to her chair. She picked up the rock and read the note. "It states they're giving me forty-eight hours to vacate and give them control of the building or I can expect those closest to me to face the consequences." Belle kept her head bowed.

Shane guessed she fought to keep her emotions under control. She couldn't come across weak. They depended on her strength and influence.

"We need men in different parts of the building, keeping watch at each window and door. Rose has been cooking all morning, so, I'm going to eat her delicious food in my room. Thanks for helping us."

Shane took Ella's hand and drew her close as she stared at him. "We'll get through this. I promise

I won't let anyone harm you." Shane had never experienced anything better. She fit into his arms perfectly and he wanted to stay this way for the rest of the night.

"You can't make any promises, Shane. I'm wise enough to know this doesn't look good for any of us."

"We wondered if we'd make it when the tornado bore down on us, but we did. Susie is waiting for you to come for her. I need you to get through this." His hand gently caressed the back of her neck.

"Forty-eight hours until we can expect to face the consequences. What does that even mean? Will we witness a gun fight in front of the bordello? Are they going to raid it during the night? None of this makes sense. We're just sitting ducks in here waiting for them to pick us off. We must do something. There has to be a way to get to Janson. We should send a telegram to your father, he may know someone who'd help."

"Not sure if my father will know anything, but you're right, we need to do something. Let's eat and talk with the men. No one had any ideas when Belle asked them, other than just watching each side of the building."

Ella laid her head on his chest. "They must have weaknesses. Everyone has faults. We need to strike them before they strike us."

"I agree. Hopefully, we can get a telegram sent to my father, and see if he will help us. Time is running out."

Chapter Thirteen

Ella stood inside the telegraph office. Clouds covered most of the sunlight trying to burst through. Two of Belle's men accompanied them into town and watched outside while Shane sent his father a message. Belle gave Ella a gun, and it laid in her bag fully loaded. No telling where Janson's gunmen were.

"Miss, you look upset. Is there anything I can do for you?" A man in a black suit came up to her. His hair mostly blonde with a little gray at the temples. The gray enhanced his strong features. Looking into his brown eyes gave Ella a sense of peace.

"I'm fine, sir."

"You don't look fine. Would you let me pray with you? I'm a traveling preacher, and my name is, Pastor Harris. I go from town to town in Colorado and extend hope to many people in painful situations. Nothing is beyond God's intervention." He steered her toward a bench a couple of feet behind them and sat next to her.

"It's a long story, and I can't explain it all, but there are some cruel men threatening to harm us. We don't know where they are, or what they will do, but we're seeking a way to stop them."

"I'm sorry. Sounds like you could use a lot of help. Do you know, Jesus?"

"I do."

"Have you sought Him for wisdom?"

"No. God's been so distant. I don't understand why He's allowed all these things to take place. I've always sought to do what He wants me to."

"He allows each of us our own free will, but if we're in the path of someone who hasn't made the best decisions, their consequences can spill over into our lives. God's still working, but the answer may not be what we'd expected. He might allow the distress you're going through, but it's never without a purpose." Pastor Harris wiped his brow.

"The telegram is sent." Shane walked toward them. He held out his hand. "We haven't met. I'm, Shane Wyatt." Pastor Harris shook his hand. Ella could tell Shane didn't trust the man.

"I'm Pastor Harris, nice to meet you, Shane. I enjoyed speaking with this lovely lady as she waited for you. I hope what I've said has helped. I'd be happy to pray for you both."

"We need to get going Pastor." Shane glanced at Ella. "Let's leave."

"We would appreciate your prayers, though." Ella gave the Pastor a brief smile.

"Of course. Blessings to you both." Pastor Harris nodded and strode toward the counter.

"Do you consider it wise talking with him?"

Shane closed the door behind them.

"He's fine. I could tell by looking in his eyes, they aren't the eyes of an evil man. I felt a sense of peace talking with him. He only wished to calm my spirit and give me hope. Something we are sorely lacking in this situation." Ella stopped and stared at Shane. "We should pay Jim Janson a visit."

"Are you thinking about what would happen if we did that? It's the last place we should go."

"I don't believe so. He won't expect us, so we'll catch him off guard."

"He won't let us leave once we're there. We'll have surrendered every bit of advantage we might have against him." Shane stopped walking and looked into her eyes. "I would love to confront him too. Have it out with him once and for all. And while that opportunity may certainly arise, I don't want to give him any help. We do need to make the first move, but we have to consider what will have the biggest impact against him."

"Our only chance is to surprise them when they least expect it." Ella looked back at the men trailing them. "His threats can't intimidate us."

Suddenly, a gunshot rang out. Ella heard something whiz past her. Shane shoved her to the ground while Belle's guards opened fire. Ella looked back in time to witness a man drop to the dirt. Their men were still standing. Shane helped her up. "Are you all right? Sorry, I had to push you down, that bullet almost hit you. We need to hurry to the brothel."

The pastor from the telegraph office came rushing toward them. "Is anybody injured?"

"No, it missed us, but it came close to Ella." Shane scanned everyone around them for more gunslingers who might wish to use them for target practice.

"Where can we take you two that's safe?" Pastor Harris stood on the other side of Ella while the guards surrounded them.

"The only place we can go is Belle's brothel." Shane watched the pastor's reaction.

"I see. Well, let's move." Pastor Harris took hold of Ella's arm and hustled her along.

When they stepped through the door of the bordello, Ella almost fainted. She sat down on a bench.

"Would you like me to get the doctor?" Pastor Harris patted her hand.

"No. I'm not hurt. Once I calm down, I should be fine."

"All right. Let's see what I can find out about the man who shot at you. If I learn something significant, I'll be back. I'm staying at the Gold Rush Boarding House." Pastor Harris glanced at Shane. "Do you need anything?"

"A few hundred men."

Pastor Harris laughed. "I'll see what I can do. I will talk with the sheriff, he needs to do something about this. His wife wouldn't want him sitting by while women are being shot at."

"Thank you, Pastor, but the Sheriff is in the back pocket of these criminals. He's had an opportunity to intervene, but hasn't." Shane sat next to Ella and pulled her close to his side.

"Hopefully, he'll listen to me." Pastor Harris

closed the door behind him as Belle walked into the room.

"Ella, are you hurt?" She rushed over to her.

"A man shot at me, but the bullet missed. I'm a little shaky. I doubt he wanted to kill us or we'd be dead. We weren't far from him. It had to be a warning."

"I can't wait until Janson and his puppets get what they deserve." Belle took hold of her hand.

A tap on the front door broke up their conversation.

"Come in," Belle yelled.

A woman stepped through the door. "There's a telegram for Mr. Wyatt. Is he here?"

Shane stood and accepted the paper from her. "Thank you, ma'am."

"Should I wait for a reply before I leave, sir?"

"Yes, of course." Shane read the wire. "I will need to answer."

"There's ink and pens in my office, Shane." Belle sat down next to Ella.

Shane left for a few minutes, then came back with a folded piece of paper. He handed it to the courier with a few coins. "Thanks for sticking around."

"You're welcome, sir." She left.

"What did your father say?" Ella stood up and walked over to Shane. He gave her the wire.

Shane,

I've heard Janson is being followed by those in our state government because of his unending supply of money and he's made many enemies. There's a string of unexplained murders in the wake of him rising to power. Some men have sought to take him down, but Janson's been untouchable. Stay clear of dealing with him. If you need help, I know a few business associates in Cripple Creek. They owe me.

"You asked him for help?"

"I did."

"Should he ask those men he's speaking of for help?" Ella's stomach did more flip flops. What did Janson have planned? Why hadn't he taken advantage of their vulnerability and lack of firepower instead of toying with them? There had to be a reason.

"My father won't wait to contact the men he knows. He's a man of action. Isn't it odd Janson's not responding as soon as he can? It's as if he's giving us time to get help. It doesn't seem right."

"I thought the same thing, Shane." Ella glanced at Belle. "Any theories?"

"I don't understand it either. Once he stole all the women from me, it would have been the perfect time for him to strike. I will send Katie over there to see if she can get anything out of the girls. All she's done is sat in her room crying. Rose took on all the duties. Katie can tell them she made a mistake and wants to work with them. Hopefully, she'll be believed, and tell us what she finds out." Belle leaned over and studied Ella. "You've lost all your color. You should take a nap? Tonight will be busy trying to come up with a plan for tomorrow."

"My stomach is upset and my head is pounding. Sending Katie over there might be a great idea. I hope she'll agree. I'll go lie down for a bit." Ella yawned.

Shane followed her to the room they'd shared last night. Ella took her shoes off and climbed up onto the bed. She sunk into the mattress and sighed in contentment. She got under the quilt then fluffed her pillow.

"Do you want me to build a fire?" Shane walked over to the hearth.

"Sure, although it might be a bit early."

"The warmth may relax you. I'll bring in more wood from outside."

"Thank you." Ella lied down. She missed her parents so much. It seemed like months since they'd left Texas, not a few weeks. Ella knew her life had changed forever, she'd never be the same girl who'd been kidnapped. She went from a naïve ranch girl to a woman who'd been in some dangerous situations.

"This should get us through the night. It's chilly in the evenings." Shane stacked the logs in the hearth with kindling underneath and lit it. "I expected you'd be asleep by now."

"My mind keeps cycling each thing we've been through and won't let me sleep."

The flame struggled at first but soon took hold as the fire consumed the wood. He sat on the bed next to Ella. "You went through all these things because of me. It's been quite the journey."

"Every decision and action we make could mean the difference between life and death." Ella sat up.

"It's crucial we think everything through."

Shane took hold of Ella's hand.

His touch brought comfort and longing. He caressed the back of her hand with his thumb.

Tingles ran up and down Ella's arm. "I might know you better than anyone else, even though we haven't been together very long. I've listened while you shared your mistakes, your hopes, and your relationships. We've been through some frightful events, yet you've been strong and compassionate. I've despised you. You took me from my family. You didn't explain what Belle did for a living. But when you touch me all those thoughts leave. The only thought left is the one which wants you to hold me. We may not survive through tomorrow, so does anything beyond this moment really matter? We're married. God doesn't care why, He looks on it as a covenant between us. A commitment that time and suffering should never separate. Will you hold me?"

"Do you understand what you're saying, Ella? If you want to annul this marriage or if your parents require you to, then the less we get involved the better. Holding you close may lead to things which might not be the best right now. I'm not the man your parents would want for you. I'd love nothing better than to be a husband to you in every way, but I worry you'd regret it."

Ella moved closer to him. She touched his hair. He turned toward her and they gazed into each other's eyes. Was he the man she believed him to be or was he the man everyone knew him to be? How could she consider a life with someone who didn't love Jesus? Although, she'd already married him, so wouldn't she be expected to honor their vows even though they weren't said for the right reasons?

"Ella, we shouldn't do this. You're young and even though we're married, you weren't ready to be married. I could get lost looking into those beautiful eyes of yours. I need to remember my purpose is protecting you, not taking advantage of your vulnerability."

Ella drew her fingers through his hair. "Do you remember the night at your parent's house when we kissed?"

"Of course, I didn't want to stop kissing you. I've thought of those moments often. You don't understand how being near you affects me. Any man would be honored to have you as his wife. Ella, you're not only pretty, but you're wise and compassionate. If I did what I wanted to, you'd probably hate me for the rest of our lives."

"Not if I want you to. Ella lightly brushed his lips with hers.

Shane kissed her passionately. He slowly ran his hands through her hair. Ella opened her eyes and studied him. Feelings beyond desire stirred at his caress. Could she love him? His kisses were so much more than she'd imagined a kiss could be. It was unexplainable. His heart beating under her hand brought comfort as he pulled her closer. She closed her eyes. Nothing else mattered but the softness of his lips on hers. He paused and kissed her cheek, then her neck, trailing kisses to her shoulder.

"Ella, I want nothing more than to continue this and see where it goes. But, I don't think we should make that choice until we're safe, not hiding out in a brothel scared we might die. It's so hard to leave you, but we can't go beyond this." He stood up. "I'm going outside to chop more wood."

It seemed as if the air had been sucked from her lungs. Coldness hit her the minute he stood up. He hadn't told Ella he loved her. If he stayed with her, she'd never leave him, but perhaps he wanted an escape. He didn't believe Ella knew what she wanted, but maybe he was the one who couldn't be sure she was enough. Shane had needed her to pay a debt, and he made a promise to take her back to Texas and that's as far as his commitment would go. Ella got up. Time to find Janson's weaknesses.

Chapter Fourteen

A branch scratched Ella's arm as she pressed through the bushes to gaze in the window. She'd bribed the desk clerk of the hotel they'd stayed at to get directions to Janson's house. Ella changed into a dress left behind by one of Belle's girls and snuck out of the brothel right after Shane went out to chop wood. The men outside had been huddled together discussing something and didn't notice her leaving. She hid the gun under her skirt, held in place with a couple of garters.

Ella stood on tiptoe trying to peek into the front room of Janson's house. It had to be the sitting room, but only lamps glowed in the empty room. Just her luck, she'd scratched herself up for nothing. A tree rose in front of the next window blocking her view. Ella had climbed many trees, but not dressed as she happened to be now. The bodice dipped lower than she felt comfortable with, but they'd assume, she was following in her mother's footsteps. If she got spotted, it would take quick thinking and a lot of deception to get out of it.

She made her way to the next window and struck gold. Two men and two women sat at a table. He must not be concerned about his plans for Belle tomorrow. The window had been left ajar to let the refreshing night air blow through. She crouched under it to hear what they were talking about.

"Well, Janson, I understand you're setting up a new business. I never dreamed it would be a brothel."

She stood up enough so she could see which man had been speaking. Janson sat closest to her.

"William, there is lots of capital to be generated. I like anything that makes me cash."

The blonde woman next to Janson placed her hand on his arm. "Jim, I don't like you dealing with those types of women."

"Ruth, I'm not working with them. I employed a fellow with quite the reputation of keeping his girls in line. He won't put up with any disobedience or they'll be dealt with." Janson patted her hand.

"Belle isn't letting go easily." William took a slurp of water.

"She believes she can stop me. Little does she realize, she's playing right into my hands. I'll get rid of her and another nasty problem I've been dealing with and no one will be the wiser," Janson laughed.

William took a bite of food. "She may be fiercer than you expect. She's hired a few pretty tough men to support her in the battle against you."

"All the better. Belle's doing precisely what I expected her to. Although, she's contacted some powerful men in Denver trying to find dirt on me. I don't like that. This has to be finished tomorrow. I anticipate having the brothel running again this week under new ownership. Poor Belle, will either be run out of town or six feet under, depending on how she reacts."

"Didn't her daughter show up?"

"She did. Bad timing on her part. Rumors are, she's quite the beauty, and is involved with that Wyatt fellow. He's one lucky guy, they were recently married. I've warned her to head back to where she came from, but she's still here. None of them are taking me seriously." Janson kissed the blonde woman next to him on the cheek. "They'd be wise to do so, wouldn't they Princess?"

She giggled nervously. "Yes, they don't understand how much you hate disobedience."

The other woman in the room looked uncomfortable, even scared. If Ella found a way to talk with her, she might learn what Janson planned but they hadn't even had dessert yet. She hadn't seen any guards around his house which didn't make sense.

"Sounds like there might be a lot of excitement tomorrow. I heard someone got killed today, although, it does seem to be a daily occurrence in our town." William smiled at Janson. "They told me the guy shot at Belle's daughter, what a coincidence."

"You're well informed. Remind me to solicit your counsel if I'm ever uncertain of what is going on in town." Janson smirked.

"Well gentlemen, it's time for cake. Enough talk

about work. We're supposed to be having a fun evening." Janson's princess rang a bell beside her plate.

"You're right, dear. Let's speak of more pleasant matters." Janson stared at William.

William had said the right words but the way his body tensed, Ella wondered if he and Janson were friends or rivals. Anger from Janson's comments made her want to march in there and confront him. Instead, she backed away from the window and bumped into someone.

"The boss doesn't appreciate people spying on him. I doubt he knew of your visit tonight." The man stood a foot taller than her.

"I heard in town he needed more women for the new business he is establishing. I wanted to see if he'd hire me. I didn't want to disturb him if he has plans, so I glanced through the window when I overheard voices inside. I decided to leave when I saw they were having a dinner party." Ella gave the man her best innocent eyes look.

"It's late, and this window is a long way from the front door. He only hires at his office. You better not come around here anymore or I'll take you in to meet him, he won't be happy."

"I won't be back, sorry to have troubled you." Ella laid her hand on his arm. "Once I'm hired, you can come down and visit."

"I don't go to those places."

"You'd make an exception for me though, right?" Ella batted her eyes and smiled.

"I'll think about it. Now, get out of here before someone else sees you and I have to take you to the boss."

"I'm disappearing right now." Ella walked as fast as she could. Her heart pounding so rapidly she worried she might faint. She'd almost made it to the street when she heard a noise and dove between the bushes. Someone grabbed her arm.

"Well, what did I find? Why are you sneaking around? Boss doesn't like anybody on his property. You're coming with me." He pulled Ella to the back of the house where the guy who'd let her go shook his head. The other man hurried her through the kitchen and into a hall where he ordered one of the servants to bring Mr. Janson.

A couple of minutes later Janson walked in scowling. "What's going on?" His eyes locked on Ella.

"I discovered this woman sneaking around the house."

"Is that right, Miss? Or should I say, Mrs. Wyatt? Your hair is the same unmistakable color as your mothers. How nice of you to pay me a visit. I'd heard Belle's daughter was beautiful, but I never imagined you'd be quite so exquisite. Married life must not keep you busy enough if you're spying for your mother dressed as a prostitute. Thinking of taking over the family business? Oh, but wait, there is no family business." Janson laughed. "It belongs to me now. I'd love to employ a beauty like you, what a boost for my business." He laughed again. "I'm going to have to figure out what to do with this gift. Lock her in the guest room at the end of the hall." Janson patted her cheek as the man grasped her arm again. He ordered the guard to stay outside her room.

"You're not going to get away with this." Ella lunged at him but the guard held her back. "Too many people are investigating you."

"Oh, feisty, like Belle too, must be that fiery red hair. A lesson your mother never taught you is, when to realize you're fighting a losing battle. There are worse situations than starting over, and your actions tell me you wish to discover what those are." Janson stepped backward. "Take her to the room. I need to get back to my guests before they wonder what's going on."

Ella screamed, but the guard clamped his hand over her mouth.

"Gag her and tie her up. I have no time for this." Janson headed down the hall.

Ella struggled to free herself from the guard's grasp as he dragged her toward the room, but it was no use. His grip dug into her arms like an iron clamp. He shoved her from the front, sending her backward onto the bed. He clamped his hand over her face pushing her head into the bedding. The force of his palm against her mouth busted her lip. She tasted blood and gasped for air as he held her down while he untied a bandana from his neck. Ella gagged as he crammed it into her mouth. Flipping her over like a rag doll, he tied it, then pulled her arms behind her back and tied them. He strapped her ankles together.

"Learning to control your mouth would have been a wise choice and a lot more comfortable. You'd best not try anything, as I'll be outside the door." He left her alone.

Ella struggled to wiggle her hands to loosen the ropes, but he'd tied them too tight. She laid there face first in the bedding. She realized coming here had achieved nothing, in fact, it had given Janson even more leverage to use against Belle.

She needed to get her hands free. *I need you, Jesus. Help me, please.* Ella's eyes overflowed with tears and they ran down her nose and onto the bed. Why hadn't she listened to Shane or Pastor Harris?

The door opened. "I ended my dinner party early so I might spend some time with you." He untied her ankles and turned her over. "Oh, tears. Are you upset?" He loosened the bandana. "You'll doubtless be more anxious later, as I don't see this ending well for your husband and mother."

Ella's lip had swollen. "What causes a man to take enjoyment in ruining other people's lives?"

"A man tired of being told what he can and can't do. So, he proves he does whatever he wants. I offered your mother a fair deal, to begin with, but she said no. She should have accepted it, but she said she'd never sell to me. It forced my hand to show how serious the consequences were to anybody who refused me." He sat down in a chair by the bed.

"Why should people relinquish everything they've worked for because you decide you want it? Why don't you build your own brothel? You've already hired most of the women from Belle." Ella glared at him.

"I don't need to build my own when what I want already exists. I would've kept your mother running the place had she wanted too if she had only sold it to me."

"Did you ever consider she didn't want to work for someone else, that's why she moved west?"

"Everyone has a story, but I only care about my own. Tomorrow, I fix two complications which have been plaguing me. I frame Belle in the death of my business associate who's been trying to take over my businesses. She goes to jail, he's dead, and the building gets confiscated and auctioned off. Mine will be the only bid. Of course, now that I've told you my intentions, I'll have to kill you. It'll look like you tried to save your mother and got shot by my associate. The sheriff will see to that. You'll die a hero. Lay back and get some rest. Your last day on earth is tomorrow." Janson stood up.

"You may assume you have this all plotted out, but events don't always go as planned. I wouldn't want to be in your place when you stand before God."

"Such a great myth, the Bible. I prefer to rely on myself rather than fictional characters. Sweet dreams." Janson left the room.

Ella laid her head back. Janson had neglected to gag her and tie her feet. Had anyone missed her at the brothel? Her stomach hurt as she considered her future. "*Yea, though I walk through the shadow of death, I will fear no evil. For thou art with me...*" Suddenly, she knew whether she survived or not, she won.

Chapter Fifteen

Shane split the last log in half. He'd been pondering his response to Ella while he chopped wood. His emotions were so conflicted, he hadn't explained his feelings well. Ella's family would not approve of him, yet he cared more for her than he'd ever had for anyone. He was falling in love with the red-haired woman who challenged him every chance she got. He needed her to love him for who he would be with her, not because she didn't know if she'd live past tomorrow. He gathered up the wood and headed back to their room.

He didn't see her when he opened their door. Ella's dress laid over the bed, so she'd changed clothes. Something didn't feel right. He strode to the kitchen and asked Rose if she'd saw her leaving. She hadn't. He hurried outside and questioned the men. They didn't either. He walked back in and searched the brothel. Belle still slept. It's as if Ella vanished.

Everyone searched the building inside and out

for any clues to where she might be. Nothing. They met in the kitchen to talk about the last time they'd all seen her.

Rose stood by the stove waiting for the water to boil. The men talked while snacking on fresh-baked cookies.

Belle sat down at the kitchen table. "Did anybody see her leaving? How did she leave without anyone noticing, you're supposed to be watching the building?

One of the men spoke up. "Yes, ma'am, but honestly, we cannot keep an eye on every part of the building with only six of us. We have to sleep, and nature calls.

"Shane, did you detect anything unusual this afternoon which might give us an understanding of what she'd been thinking?"

Shane almost choked on the water he'd just swallowed. How could he honestly answer that question? She'd been upset because he said he couldn't be with her. The guys in the room would laugh and think what a fool he must be.

"Ella had been very upset. I tried calming her down, but it didn't help. I went outside to chop wood so she could sleep and when I came back in, she'd disappeared."

"Did she talk about meeting anybody?" Belle reached for the cup of tea Rose gave her.

"No, not that I recall. I don't understand why her dress would be on the bed. She didn't bring many clothes and they are in her bags. What did she wear? It had to be something left behind from the girls. Why would she wear one of their dresses?"

Shane added sugar to the coffee, Rose, sat before him.

"If she needed to dress like one of my girls, she had a reason. There isn't much time before Janson makes a move and now Ella's missing. If a couple of the guys will go with me, I'm paying the sheriff a visit. He hasn't listened to me yet, but maybe Ella disappearing will change his mind." Belle stood up, grabbed her shawl and joined the men heading out the door. The other four went outside too.

Rose sat next to Shane. He was struggling to recall what had been said between them. Before Ella had been shot at, she wanted to go to Janson and confront him. Surely, she didn't go there alone. It might explain her trying to pose as a prostitute. He assumed Ella had given up on going there, but when she got upset, she probably wanted to prove him wrong.

Shane glanced at Rose. "I figured out where she is. She spoke earlier about confronting Janson. After being shot at I'd presumed she'd decided it would be a bad idea. But, it's the only explanation that makes sense."

"Why would she confront him, especially after what happened this afternoon? He'd take her hostage, use her as leverage to get what he wants from Belle. I hope you're wrong." Rose shook her head.

"I do too, but I have a suspicion I'm not."

Rose stirred the stew she started earlier and pulled apples out of a cupboard. "Keeping busy helps me not dwell on everything's that's going on. Gonna make an apple pie."

"Has Katie been back since she left to meet with the girls?"

Rose sliced apples. "No, and I fear she won't. She wanted a reason to join them. She's scared we're all going to get killed. If we make it out of this alive, I'm finished with this way of life. I should have gotten out long ago.

Once Belle found out where Ella lived she wanted to sell everything and go there but then she got sick. She's tired of being a madam. At one point, she'd been so driven by money she almost forgot what mattered. Something happened, and she went back to the way she'd always been. I never discovered what, but I was glad it did. In this type of business, there isn't much good. When you're around the vilest of people, you become them. I'm not proud of the life I've led. I want a fresh start and a family someday but only if I can find a man who really cares, like you."

Rose stirred the apples in cinnamon and sugar and added them to a pie crust she made. "Nothing better than apple pie."

"Yes, it's Ella's favorite. Someone will snatch you right up and be very happy he did. I doubt the sheriff is going to do anything. I've got to find Ella before anything happens to her. She wouldn't be in this mess if I hadn't kidnapped her. We've all made plenty of mistakes so I'm the last one to judge you. It's taken me this long to realize I need to change."

The back door opened and shut. Belle walked in. "This town's sheriff is about as much of a lawman as our tabby cat. He's scared of his shadow and even more so of Janson. He ain't going to do anything."

"Shane has a theory of where Ella may be." Rose pulled out a chair for Belle.

"I remember before the gunfire started she tried to persuade me to confront Janson. I thought she'd given up on going to his home but now it's the only idea which makes sense. She might've dressed up as a prostitute in case she got caught."

"If Janson's got Ella, I doubt he'll hurt her. He will use her against me to get everything he's after. The girl has spunk, reminds me of myself. I'm so tired." Belle massaged her temples. "I can't do much more tonight. My head aches."

Belle got up. "I am so weak. We're never as invincible as we believe we are. When I finally get the chance to be there for my daughter, my body won't cooperate."

"I'm sorry, Belle. I know how much you've wanted to spend time with Ella. It's not right what Janson is doing to you." Rose placed the pie in the oven. "He'll pay for what he's doing."

"Don't I know it? Every bad decision I made is hurting me now. At night I dread falling asleep because of my dreams. This brothel is like an empty tomb since all the girls left. I hear screaming and crying in the middle of the night but no one's here. I wanted to sell this building to have money to help Ella, but her life is worth more than wealth. I devoted my life to the wrong things, first by selling myself, and later others. I had no idea what it would take from me. My one chance at happiness had been with Ella's father, and I threw it away. The lure of easy money pulled me back, and I convinced myself

I had to take care of everyone.

In reality, I did it for the drugs I'd been taking since I was fourteen. The woman I'd worked for made certain I had them each day. In the beginning, they numbed what the men did to me, they let me escape from reality for a time. Eventually, I had to have the drugs, or I'd get really sick. They almost killed me. It took everything within me to give them up, but I did. My bad choices contributed to ailments that are ravaging my body and stealing time away with my daughter." Belle's left leg buckled, and she almost collapsed. "It's cruel but I can't change it."

"Let's take you to your room." Shane lifted her arm around his shoulders and nearly carried her up the stairs. She weighed nothing. Rose opened Belle's bedroom door.

She took off Belle's shoes and drew the quilt over her as they got her into the bed. "I'll send one of the men for the doctor."

"It's so cold." Belle's teeth chattered.

"I'll get wood and build a fire. Good thing I chopped lots earlier" His mind reeled as he processed what Belle had said. The life she'd led brought her to this place of regret. The intensity of her sorrow shook him. Belle never found happiness, only illness, and heartache. She'd been given a chance to leave a childhood of heartaches and find contentment with a man she loved and their baby girl, but because of the drugs, Belle lost them both.

Shane realized his gambling had him on a similar path. He hadn't wanted to play cards since he came back to Cripple Creek, but he'd been busy.

He wanted a family and risking money on card games wouldn't be a part of it. He grabbed an armload of wood, rushed up the stairs to Belle's room. He had the fire roaring in no time. Rose sat by Belle's bedside waiting for the doctor. Belle's gentle snores filled the room.

"I've got to see if I can find Ella. I'm taking a couple of men with me. Do you need anything before I take off?"

"We'll be fine. Belle did too much today, hopefully, she'll be good in the morning. You need to find Ella." Rose sat back in the chair. "I'll probably stay in here tonight."

"She's lucky to have you."

"Belle was there for me at a really tough time in my life. She offered me a place to live, food to eat, and a roof over my head. I could've left at any point, but we've become friends. She's confided in me, and I've come to realize she has a lot of value in her heart. It's the least I can do for her."

"It speaks well as to your character, a lot of people would've left her. I hope to be back with Ella soon."

~

Shane hid behind barrels in an alley across from Janson's. There hadn't been any action outside the house. The two men who'd joined him had split up and were trying to get close enough to look inside or overhear any conversations.

He didn't know what their next step should be. If Ella was inside they needed to get her out before something bad happened.

One of the guys walked up to Shane. "I haven't seen or heard anything out of the ordinary. Janson's men are sitting around a fire near the house. None of them are talking about finding a woman on the property. I suggest we go home for the night and come back in the morning."

"If Ella's in there, we need to get her out."

"I understand your hurry, but they have a huge advantage, especially at night. We can't tell how many men are inside, but there's about fifteen outside. They could quickly kill her before we even got close."

Shane looked at the house. "If I leave it feels like I'm giving up on her. But you're right, attempting to get in there would be a massacre. If Ella is in there, there is no way to get her out tonight. We're of no use to them, they'd as soon shoot us as look at us. My gut tells me she's in there. I promised, Belle, I'd bring her back, now I am giving up." He motioned to the other man to come back over. "Let's leave. Who knows what tomorrow holds? We gotta be ready for anything."

Shane glanced at the house, then turned and followed the men. Failure settled on his shoulders, the heavy weight caused his body to slump forward. He should've handled this afternoon better. With each step he sensed the darkness devouring him. Sleep would be a long time in coming tonight.

"Mr. Wyatt."

"Shane turned his head." Pastor Harris emerged from the blackness.

"Where did you come from?"

"I spoke to the men at the brothel and they said Ella's missing. They mentioned you suspect she came here. Did you see her?

"No, we didn't see or hear her." Shane dropped his head.

"You've taken Ella's safety upon yourself, haven't you?"

"Yes, I brought her here, initially against her will. If I hadn't, her life wouldn't be in danger. She'd be happy with her family."

"Have you ever considered God has a plan for each of our lives?"

"I haven't thought much about Him. Don't even know if I believe God is real."

Pastor Harris set his hand on Shane's shoulder as they walked. "I used to believe the same thing. Now, I have no doubt there is a God. He took me from the mess of a life I'd created for myself and gave me a reason to live. We're never really alone. He's waiting for us to give everything to Him, these burdens are too big to carry on our own. You'll never measure up, none of us can, thankfully, we never have to. Don't wait too long, son."

Shane didn't know how to respond. When Pastor Harris came along beside him the darkness which had engulfed him departed. "I'll think about it."

"Good. I'm going back to the hotel to pray for God's grace and mercy in this situation, and a miracle or two wouldn't hurt either. If you need to talk to me anytime, I'd consider it an honor." Pastor Harris turned and strolled away.

Shane had almost made it back to the brothel.

Could there be a God who cared for him and Ella? The image prompted a welcomed sense of comfort. He wondered if Ella might be praying. There were no clouds in the sky only a thousand twinkling stars sparkling in the night. *God, if you're real, we need a miracle.*

As Shane got to the back door of the brothel something caught his eye. A piece of paper wrapped around a rock. Another note. He took it inside and read it in the dim candlelight.

Belle,
Meet me at the home of my partner, Stan Hall, at two tomorrow. Make sure you're alone and that you bring the deed to the building and a thousand dollars or you'll never see your daughter alive again.
Jim Janson

Chapter Sixteen

Janson's man cut the ropes that tied Ella's hands together. "Wake up. The boss is ready to leave, and you're coming with us."

"I need to use the outhouse." Trying to stand after being in the same position all night shot tingles up and down her legs. She'd fallen asleep from sheer fatigue.

"You'll have to hurry." The guy pulled her down the hallway and outside to the door of the outhouse.

"You'd be a fool to try anything."

Once she finished, he rushed her toward a carriage waiting by the back door. He shoved her in and sat next to her. Two men on horseback waited for Janson to give the go ahead.

Janson came out of the house a few minutes later and climbed into the carriage. "I must say, my dear, you're looking a little frazzled. Did you not sleep well? We should be in for quite the interesting afternoon. I hope Belle has everything I've demanded."

Ella gazed out the window and ignored Janson as they traveled. He wanted her to respond to his insults so he could gloat over her misery. She wouldn't give him the satisfaction. She hoped Belle didn't come. A two-story home came into view and the carriage halted outside the front door. The sunlight pierced a hole between white puffy clouds and warmed her skin. It seemed strange thinking normal thoughts when she may not live through this day. God had given her peace through this whole ordeal. Nothing else could explain how she'd remained calm.

Janson spoke to the man next to Ella. "Today, if all goes as planned, my business partner of fifteen years will pay for the transgressions he's committed against me. I trusted him, and he stole from me. He'll soon not be a problem, and I'll have gained a successful brothel and a hefty sum of money. Gag her. We can't have her warning anyone."

Janson opened the carriage door while the gunslinger shoved a bandana in her mouth and tied it. "Let's get you inside before your mother arrives." He grabbed Ella's arm and tugged her outside.

A bird sang in the distance, the only sound in the silence of this eerie setting. The man grasped Ella's arm as Janson knocked on the door. The butler answered and showed them to a sitting room. Janson paced. Ella sat on an elegantly upholstered chair with Janson's guard staring at her from his post. The softness of the cushions was amazing compared to what she'd slept on last night. The echo of footsteps became louder as a well-dressed gray-haired man came into the room.

"Good day, Stanley, you're looking nervous." Janson shook his hand. "Miss Fletcher should be here any time."

"I'm not comfortable with this meeting taking place here, Jim. Why didn't we meet where we normally do?" Stanley walked to the window and stared out.

"I needed it to be private. No chance of anybody coming along and disrupting our transaction. Soon she'll be handing over the deed to her property and a thousand dollars. I don't expect there will be any trouble, but one never can be too confident. Belle knows a number of men in this town. They might help her out more than I've given her credit for."

Ella struggled to warn Stanley with her eyes that Janson was a liar but he wouldn't look at her. Janson was plotting his murder and setting her mother up to get the blame.

A knock on the door interrupted the pleasantries. The butler showed Belle into the room. Ella and she exchanged glances. Belle's complexion looked almost white, and her breathing seemed labored.

"If it isn't the lady of the hour. You know, I thought your daughter looked bad today, but I have to say you look much worse." Janson snickered. "This shouldn't take long. I assume you brought the deed and the cash?"

Belle handed Janson some papers and the bag she'd been carrying. "It's all there. I'll be taking my daughter now and I don't ever want to see you again. If I do, it'll be the last time." Belle stared at Stanley. "If you're in business with this man, I'd think twice. He only cares about one thing, himself."

Suddenly, a gunshot rang out, and the window shattered from a bullet. Shards of glass flew and broke all over the floor. In the midst of the chaos, Janson fired his revolver at his business partner. Stanley grabbed his chest and fell with a thud. Belle immediately pushed Ella to the ground shielding her with her body. Bullets blasted through walls sending wood fragments flying through the air. Belle and Ella frantically scooted along the floor and under a desk. Voices yelling outside were indistinguishable because of the gunfire. Bullets continued to rain, knocking items from shelves, and pictures from walls. Ella scanned the room for Janson, but he was nowhere to be seen. The man who had been guarding her had disappeared. Stanley lay in a pool of blood, and Ella watched him gasp his final breath. Just as swiftly as it began, silence fell. Belle glanced at Ella. "Honey, we've got to get out of here. I hope my men have taken care of everybody." Belle untied her gag. Ella scrambled to her feet, adrenaline pumping as she pulled Belle up with her.

As they moved toward the door, Janson stepped out from behind a bookshelf, his gun drawn, pointing right at Belle.

"I instructed you to come alone, Belle. You're gonna die, but I want to prolong your suffering by taking this pretty daughter from you." Janson turned his gun toward Ella and pulled the trigger, but not before Belle jumped in front of her.

"No!" Ella screamed.

The bullet struck Belle, and she crumpled to the floor. The door burst open, and one of Belle's men opened fire on Janson.

Shane came rushing in, his gun drawn. Pastor Harris followed behind.

"Belle, we've eliminated the threats outside. Belle?"

Pastor Harris saw her on the ground. "No! Belle!" He squatted beside her and checked her pulse. "She has a bullet wound to the chest, but she's alive. We need to get her to a doctor."

Shane checked Janson and Stanley's pulse. They were both dead.

The men carried Belle to the carriage. They laid her on one of the benches. Shane gave Pastor Harris his shirt to apply pressure to the wound. Ella sat across from her and held her hand. Shane jumped up front on the bench with the driver.

"Go!" Shane yelled as he shook the reigns signaling the horses to take off, pulling the carriage away from the house.

Even though Belle was conscious, she had scarcely made any noise since getting shot. She'd moaned a couple of times when they lifted her into the carriage.

Pastor Harris gripped Ella's other hand. "Will you pray with me?"

Ella bowed her head as Pastor Harris prayed.

When they finished, Belle opened her eyes and turned her head toward Pastor Harris.

"Your voice, it's so familiar to me."

"It's me, Belle. I've been keeping track of you for many years, traveling between mining towns in Colorado. I watched you from afar, making sure you were alright."

Belle coughed. "Robert… you must hate me." Belle chocked, blood ran from the corner of her mouth. "Ella, this is your father."

Ella gasped. Her mind understood the words but her heart couldn't believe them.

Pastor Harris looked into Ella's eyes. "It's true, Ella. I planned on telling you, but was unsure if you'd believe me." He bent toward Belle. "It's true I resented you for many years, Belle. I blamed you for everything wrong in my life, including having to give Ella up. But I found forgiveness and a love so deep in Jesus. He helped me understand I should've fought harder for you and Ella. I gave up on you too soon. I forgave you and myself a long time ago, Belle, but I never approached you because I assumed you despised me. I considered it a just punishment for me to love you from afar. You need to forgive yourself and let God's love comfort you."

"God could never love me." Belle turned her head toward Ella. "Forgive me, someday."

"He's always loved you. Neither of us ever stopped loving you." Pastor Harris touched her hand. "Let us pray with you."

"I didn't think I could forgive you, but I already have." Ella squeezed her hand. "You living is what matters. You saved my life. Thank you."

"I'm not gonna make it, Ella." She coughed multiple times, tears flowing from her eyes. "I'd hoped to have more time… find the hidden box."

Ella shook her shoulders. "You need to ask God's forgiveness."

"Jesus, please… forgive me…" Belle's body went limp.

"She's gone." Pastor Harris put his arm around Ella.

A profound sadness overtook Ella. This woman gave birth to her, but she'd never known her. Belle saved her life, but she almost lost it because of her. She didn't hate her, she felt numb. Ella didn't understand Belle's choices, but she heard her reasons.

Pastor Harris took Ella's hand. "We'll need to make arrangements for her funeral."

"You knew her much better than I did." How could the father who left her at an orphanage be sitting beside her as a pastor? Both parents she'd assumed were dead had come back to her. Why didn't Pastor Harris search for her? He never stopped loving Belle. If she hadn't come to Cripple Creek, she would have never known.

The carriage swayed and bounced over the rough road. On the way to the meeting place, she hadn't even noticed. She'd been consumed in the fear of what awaited her. Now the silence inside the carriage roared inside her head. So much not said, so many years wasted. Neither of them wishing to open old wounds in reverence to the woman who lay dead in front of them. For the first time since Ella met Belle, the expression on her face was peaceful.

When they stopped in front of the brothel, Shane opened the carriage door. "Is she…"

Pastor Harris looked as if he'd aged ten years in the last few moments. Every wrinkle on his face pronounced. "She's gone."

Shane helped Ella down. "I'll have someone get the undertaker. Two men left to get the sheriff. Rose can tell the other women." He took her hand in his. The warmth of his touch on her cold hand shocked her and she jumped. "Let's go inside and get a fire going. Are you all right? Should I send for the doctor?"

"I'm fine. Only more confused now than ever. It doesn't seem real. Belle saved my life." Ella glanced at Shane. "Pastor Harris is my father."

"What!?"

"Yes, Belle recognized his voice and asked if it was him before she died. I can't even cry. I'm numb." They stepped into the room they'd shared.

"You've been through so much. A sedative might help you sleep." Shane helped her to bed, took her shoes off, and then pulled the covers over her. "I'll be back to check on you."

"I need you to sit here. I don't feel safe being alone."

Chapter Seventeen

They held the service for Belle at the Cripple Creek cemetery. Her favorite quilt draped over the casket, the only possession she had from her mother. It had saved her from freezing when Belle slept on the streets of New York City at only fourteen years of age. The edges were frayed and there were a few holes but the simple quilt laid in stark contrast to Belle's life. She'd been a woman both feared and respected. She stood her ground but lost her footing. Her roots, the connections to family, were forgotten as drugs claimed all she had. She sought to right the wrongs at the end, but her memory will forever be shrouded in sorrow for what might have been.

Many of those deemed the town's worst sinners came, none of those who considered the town better off without her had. Shane saw curtains move aside as the cart which carried her casket went down the street. Pastor Harris spoke of a woman who demonstrated why it's never too late to change.

Belle had come to this awareness in time to try to build relationships long forgotten. She gave everything to save her daughter, a selfless act of love which proved she figured out what was important. She asked God for forgiveness before Satan collected his most coveted prize. She'd been rescued from his grasp as life ebbed from her body. Now she stands before God, blameless, healed and loved.

Shane watched Ella, the tears she'd been unable to shed, now ran down her cheeks. He held her hand and understood her pain was not for what she'd lost, but what she'd never really had. He observed everyone and wondered if they comprehended the words Pastor Harris spoke. Shane's palms were sweaty and God's unseen love tugged at his heart until he imagined it being pulled from his chest. Did everybody understand the magnitude of this moment?

Pastor Harris asked if anybody would like to take the step Belle had. Shane tried to sit still, but he wanted to run into the love the Pastor spoke of. Nothing had ever meant more than this moment. Shane looked around. There were five people raising their hands. He lifted his. The rest of the service was a blur, he couldn't wait to start this new life.

~

People brought food to Belle's Place. Ella sat next to Shane as he ate in the crowded kitchen and dining area.

"I'm happy for you," she whispered.

"Why?" Shane glanced at her.

"The decision you made today. You'll never be the same."

"I hope not. I can't describe it. I'd never considered myself worthy of God's mercy until now."

Ella sat her plate down. "So, where do we go from here?"

"We need to hire a lawyer to pay any debts Belle owed and to secure the transfer of the property to you. They'll place the building up for sale and you'll receive whatever funds are left after everybody is paid." Shane watched as Pastor Harris mingled with people who'd attended the funeral.

"Would your father take care of all of this for me?"

"I expect he would. We'll ask him when we get to Denver. Have you spoken with Pastor Harris yet?"

"Briefly. It seems like he's avoiding me. Pastor Harris must be struggling with what to say to a daughter he left at an orphanage twenty years ago. Especially now that he's a pastor, how does he explain it?"

"He's changed. I'm not the same man even after a few hours. He probably told himself you were better off without him and would hate him for leaving you behind. We haven't heard his story yet. Give him a chance to explain."

Ella laid her head back against the chair and closed her eyes.

Shane took a deep breath. "I presume you'll

want our marriage annulled. My father can take care of it. I could never apologize enough for the heartbreak I've brought to your life."

"Can we talk about this later? I can't handle anything else right now."

"Of course." Shane picked up her plate and his and took them to the sink where Rose washed dishes.

"Ella's not doing well, is she?"

"No, and I don't blame her. It's as if she'd been given a gift, and when she opened it, it was empty. Everyone has let her down in one respect or another."

Rose wiped her brow. "Have you decided what you are going to do?"

"First, I'll take Ella back to Texas and face her family. I need to confess everything to them. They may want to have me put in jail for kidnapping their daughter." Shane glanced at his boots.

"You shouldn't have kidnapped, Ella, but I doubt they'll put you in jail. You've tried to make it right and protect her. You were desperate, and you never hurt her. Plus, she met her birth parents and you're her husband now."

"Who knows for how long? They may have me arrested but I'm through running from the consequences of my actions. Are you leaving Cripple Creek?"

Rose paused from washing. "Some people interested in purchasing the brothel and turning it into a hotel came by earlier. They offered to let me run it but I'm done with this town. It'll be tough starting over, but I want to open a restaurant. I love cooking."

"I'm happy for you, Rose. You'll do well."

"I'm leaving tomorrow for Montana."

"I suppose this is goodbye then. You deserve happiness."

Rose hugged him. "Thank you, you do too."

Shane glanced at Ella, she didn't look happy. She might assume he liked Rose but what did it matter? They'd soon be annulling their marriage of protection, anyway.

A long walk should clear his head. He should pray. He had no idea how, but he reckoned he'd just talk to God like he did anybody else.

~

Darkness had enveloped the town as he returned from his walk. The moon hid behind clouds which threatened rain. He opened the door to the room he'd been sharing with Ella. A fire blazed in the hearth and the warmth made him sleepy. Ella laid in her bed looking comfortable under the blankets.

He sat on his bed. "I can move to a different room. There's no reason to pretend this marriage is real. We agreed to marry for your protection. It didn't work too well."

"It wasn't your fault that I wandered right into Janson's hands. I'd hoped to figure out their next move, but they caught me before I could get off the property. If I had made it back to the brothel, it would've saved so many lives." Ella stared into his eyes. "Do you have feelings for Rose?"

"You can't blame yourself. No. I wish her well

and she deserves a happy life, but that's the extent of my sentiments for her." Shane got up and put another chunk of wood on the fire. "Did anything happen here after I left?"

"No. Everyone looked uncomfortable and unsure of what to say to me. They don't have any idea what kind of person I am, so it was awkward."

"I can imagine. When are you wanting to leave Cripple Creek? When we stay in Denver, I'll ask my father if he would handle the legalities concerning the transfer of the brothel to you. You should wire your parents and tell them you're coming and that you'll have Susie and me with you." Shane sat back on his bed.

"The sheriff asked to meet with me tomorrow, so hopefully the day after we can leave. I wonder if Pastor Harris wants any of Belle's things. I should go through her personal items." Ella sat up. "Wait! I have to search her room!"

"What for?"

"Before Belle died, she mentioned a hidden box. She didn't give any clues as to where it is. Hopefully, in her room." Ella grabbed the lantern off the table. She still had her dress on, so she slipped on her shoes. "Will you help me search?"

"Let's go."

When they got to Belle's room, it took a while for Shane to light another lamp and get a fire burning in the hearth. The cold and the memories made him shiver, to think he'd brought Belle up here a few nights ago and now she'd never walk through her door again. Everything in life could change in a moment.

Ella removed all the books from the shelves. Rose overheard the noise and came in to ask what they were doing. Once they informed her, she searched too. They spent the next few hours exploring every inch of the room but didn't find it.

"Rose, are there any other areas of this building where Belle spent a lot of time?" Shane sat down in an armchair.

"I don't think so. She lived up here most of the time or out in the garden." Rose sneezed. "There's so much dust in here."

Ella put the rug back in place after checking the floor for loose boards. "There's a garden?"

"There is. You can't see it from the back yard, because it's across the alley behind a tall wall."

Ella hugged Rose. "I'm so glad you haven't left yet, we would've never known. I bet that's where it is. Her room would be too predictable. We'll look first thing in the morning."

"My train doesn't leave until late afternoon, so I'll help you." Rose stood up.

"Well, let's try to sleep." Shane blew out the lantern. The fire had faded to a few coals. Rose retired to her room.

Shane stopped at the bottom of the stairs on their way back to the room. "You never answered my question earlier."

Ella grabbed his hand. "I don't want to be alone. I'm uncertain of the future, but we are husband and wife and I need you to stay in the room. I can't shake the feeling someone still wants to hurt me."

"Jesus is with you." Shane put his arm around her shoulder.

"My, how things have changed." Ella opened the door to their room.

"Yes, they have."

Chapter Eighteen

Ella snuggled into her shawl. Early mornings were always chilly near the Rocky Mountains. She hadn't slept last night wondering if they'd find the box and what the contents could be. Ella and Rose waited in anticipation as Shane turned the key in the lock of the iron gate and yanked it open. Vines hung down the front, helping to camouflage it. They walked through the gate and found a sanctuary in the midst of this dirty, smelly town. Rose bushes lined a narrow path that meandered down through the middle. Smaller trails ventured off joining a pathway that encircled the outer edges of the garden. Tall trees provided shade and vining bushes covered the four walls which enclosed the oasis. Grass, flowers and a small pond took up the area in between the walkways. It was wonderful, Belle's escape from the sordid reality that had been her life.

Shane walked with the women, exploring each path. "No one would ever believe this little sanctuary would be in the middle of Cripple Creek. Its beauty should help sell the property as a hotel.

What a wonderful place for guests to enjoy. How did Belle keep it looking so nice?"

"There's a well over there behind that tree." Rose motioned across the grass. "She employed a gardener to tend to the plants and keep everything watered. This was her one luxury, where she allowed herself to forget about everything and enjoy living. It kept her sane in her insane work. I've sat with her here a few times, we chatted about our dreams and imagined what we would do if we could do anything." Rose picked a couple of tulips.

"I'd love to take the whole garden back to Texas. My family would cherish it. It reveals a side of Belle very few saw." Ella strolled around the beautiful plants while talking to Shane and Rose. "We should name the garden after her. How about Garden Belles? We could hang a sign on the gate."

"Sounds like a great idea." Shane glanced up in the trees. "Rose, any ideas where she might have stashed the box?"

"I don't, I thought about it all night. I never saw her digging or planting out here."

The gate creaked as a stooped old man shuffled into the garden. "This is private property folks, can I help you?"

"Hi, I'm Belle's daughter." Ella walked toward him.

"Names, Will. Been taking care of this garden for ten years. I couldn't make it to Belle's funeral but I fear what might happen to this place now that she's gone." He hobbled over and shook Ella's hand.

"We've heard someone wants to purchase the

property and turn the brothel into a hotel. I am going to require any owner to keep the garden as is and to call this sanctuary, Garden Belle's, after her." Ella hoped he knew about the hidden box.

"Garden Belles... I like that. Glad it will be turned into a hotel. I never liked what Belle had going on here. I loved the plants too much to let them waste away, so I stayed on for her. I'll miss Belle. Never met anyone nicer, and she enjoyed gardening as much as I do. Not many of us out here who care about such things."

"I'm sure she appreciated everything you did to make it look so beautiful. Did she ever mention a box she may have hidden out here?" Ella watched his face as she asked the question.

"Belle loved to garden. She wasn't scared of getting down in the dirt and planting flowers. I don't recall her ever digging a hole and hiding a box though. But, if she had, she'd have put it toward the back of the garden where we hadn't covered all the ground yet. Or come to think of it, she had me build a storage cabinet a while ago where she could keep her gardening tools. I never got into it, had no need to, plus she kept it locked. She planted a climbing rose in front of it that's grown up and completely concealed it. You wouldn't even notice it's there." Will walked to the area in the back. The three of them followed. He pulled branches away to expose a cabinet.

"I don't have a key."

Rose glanced at Will. "I've never seen a key other than the one to the gate."

Shane crouched and inspected the lock. "We'll

have to break it off. Much faster than searching for a key."

"Let me get some tools." Will hobbled back up the path.

"I'll carry them back." Shane followed Will through the gate.

Ella sat down and held the lock. It wouldn't take a big key to open it. She swept the dirt away next to the cabinet with her hand, her eyes intently searching for metal. The sunlight glistened on something shiny peeking out from the back corner of the cabinet. The soil had almost concealed it. She dug her fingers around and pulled out a small key. She put it in the rusty lock and it clicked open. "I found it!"

Rose came running from looking at one of the rose bushes and knelt next to Ella. "This is so exciting."

Ella took the lock off and opened the door. A few tools cluttered two narrow shelves and at first glance, disappointment settled over her, but this had to be the place. She reached in and moved her hand across the bottom shelf. She touched something toward the back. Ella pulled out a small dusty cardboard box. "This has to be it, Rose."

Ella removed the lid and discovered a bunch of papers. Should she wait for Shane and Will to return? The suspense became too great and she unfolding the first sheet, a deed to a gold mine. The second the deed to the brothel and the property it set on. A third folded paper contained receipts. They were payments made to various schools in New York City. Ella didn't understand what this meant.

A handwritten sheet of paper laid at the bottom. Opening it, she realized Belle had told her story.

I hope the person who finds this letter will be honest in how they handle this information. I bore two daughters in my early twenties. The older one was dropped off at The Children's Aid Society, an orphanage in New York City, by her father, Robert Murphey, when she was three. Her name is, Ella Murphey. I left Robert with my oldest daughter, Ella, when she was two and went back into the business of prostitution as a madam. I refused to sell myself any longer but didn't mind selling other women. I had no idea I was pregnant with our second child when I left.

I had another baby girl, Sara, and employed a woman who had children of her own to care for her. I refused to have her grow up where I worked. I visited her as often as I could. Once she became old enough to go to school, I sent her to the best boarding schools in New York City. I've provided for her and made sure she had gifts on her birthdays and at Christmas. I stayed in touch by writing her letters and visited whenever I could. She isn't aware of what I've done for a living so this will be a shock for her. My excuse has been I traveled training teachers when they were assigned to new schools out west. I'd promised to move her out by me once she graduated from college. I wanted to move to California and live a normal life by the time she finished her schooling. She never liked me being away but resigned herself to it. She doesn't consider me a good parent because I'm gone so much. I told her that her father died. I'm sorry. I couldn't come up with anything else to explain his absence. She isn't aware she has a sister, as I might not be able to locate, Ella. I've tried for a few years with no luck.

What possessions I own I want to be sold and given to my two daughters, if they both are alive and can be found. If not, it will go to the daughter still living. If neither daughter is alive, it should be divided between all their children. If there aren't any children or grandchildren, then my husband would inherit my property. His name is, Robert Murphey. My youngest daughters name is, Sara Murphey. She is attending the New York School for Young Women in New York City her headmistress is Eleanor Augusta. If there aren't any living relatives than I wish the money to be given equally to the women working for me. These are the wishes for my estate. Signed: Belle Lillian Murphey (alias Fletcher) this twenty-fifth day of August in the year of our Lord eighteen-ninety-five.

Ella glanced up from the papers. A tear rolled down her cheek.

Rose had been reading it with her. "You have a sister." Rose hugged her. "How amazing. She will need you to get through all this."

Shane and Will were walking toward them. They stared at the papers lying in her lap.

Ella looked at Shane. "I have a sister."

"Really? Where is she?"

"This letter from Belle states, she's attending a boarding school in New York. When Belle left my father, she was pregnant with her. Here read this."

"This is incredible. Did she tell you, Rose?"

"I had no idea. Although, Belle, did make trips to New York every year or two. I assumed she had friends there. None of us spoke much about our pasts."

"Doesn't your train leave soon, Rose? I'm sure we've kept you from getting ready. We need to send someone to find Pastor Harris. He needs to be told about this."

"I hope you'll keep in touch and let me know what is going on." Rose's eyes shimmered with unshed tears.

Ella smiled. "Of course. I want to hear how you're doing too. We'd love to have you settle in Texas if Montana doesn't turn out to be what you hoped. I would've never found this without you and Will. I owe you both, and plan on rewarding you for your faithfulness to Belle when this is all straightened out."

"You don't need to do nothing for me. I was just doing my job and Belle paid me well." Will followed them out the gate.

"You're a special man, Will." Shane locked the gate to the garden. They waved goodbye to Will as he hobbled away.

The three of them made their way to the back door of the brothel and went inside.

"I guess it's time to say goodbye to you both." Rose hugged them. "I hope we see each other again."

"I'll help you get your bags to the train depot." Shane smiled.

"Thank you. I'll be right back." Rose left the kitchen.

Shane put his arm around Ella and pulled her close. "Your strength amazes me. One revelation after another, and you keep moving forward." He kissed her on the forehead. "This news changes your life, yet again."

Ella melted into his arms. Strong? Her legs felt as if they'd buckle at any moment. This man made her heart race but calmed her nerves at the same time. Shane had been with her every step of the way, as he'd promised. Her parents might take a lot of convincing to see he was no longer the same person who kidnapped her but she couldn't imagine her life without him.

Chapter Nineteen

Ella stepped off the train. The view reminded her of the first time she set foot in Texas. She was a twelve-year-old orphan and arrived with her orphan friend, Laura, and their agent, Anna. Anna later adopted her and married Joshua Brown. She loved her mother and father.

Now she stood here having arrived in Texas with an orphan girl named, Susie, hanging on her arm. Life had come full circle. Ella and Susie waited on the platform as Shane got off behind them. Ella searched the crowd of people standing around and spotted her parents. She'd sent a few telegrams informing them she was alright, and not to worry, but she didn't even scratch the surface as to what had taken place while she had been in Colorado. They'd have a lot of questions and Shane would not be greeted warmly.

Ella ran to her parents pulling Susie behind her. Her father drew her into a bear hug and she wondered if he'd ever let go. "I'm so glad you're home."

Tears filled her mother's eyes when she hugged her. "We've never been so relieved to see someone step down from a train. It's been awful not knowing much of what was going on with you. Of course, we want to hear it all, but let's wait until we get to the ranch and you can tell everybody at once. Clint wanted to come with us, but I told him it would be better if you spoke with him later, as we wished to be alone with you. We haven't mentioned you're married. There was no way to break that type of news to him, it needs to come from you."

"Yes, thank you, mother. I was hoping only you and father would be here to greet us when we arrived. It would've been very awkward for me if Clint had come."

Her mother hugged her again while she whispered in her ear. "Ella, he came to us while you were gone and asked if he could have your hand in marriage. We said yes. He planned on asking you when you returned."

Ella whispered back. "I realized I never loved him in that way." She smiled at her mother as their hug ended.

"Mother, I need for you to give Shane a chance.

"He has a lot to prove." Joshua no longer looked happy.

Ella turned around and waved them over. "This is my husband, Shane Wyatt, and this beautiful little girl is, Susie McClennan. Susie and I have a lot in common. She's an orphan just like I was and so excited to see the ranch and meet everyone. I've told her lots about you all."

"Hi Susie, I'm Anna Brown, Ella's mother. And this is Joshua Brown, Ella's father. You're such a pretty girl." Anna leaned over and took Susie's hand. "We have lots of children at the ranch who will want to meet you."

Shane stood back until she finished. He stepped forward and put his hand out but Joshua didn't shake it. So he let it drop to his side. "I would appreciate it if I can speak with you privately, Mr. Brown, after Ella and I explain all that took place."

Joshua glared at Shane. "We'll for sure be talking."

"Yes, sir. Ella, I'll go get our bags." Shane touched her shoulder. "Where should I meet you?"

"Wagon's over there." Joshua nodded toward the brown wagon with two chestnut horses hitched to it.

"Beautiful horses." Shane strode to the train car where they were unloading bags.

Ella followed her parents to the wagon. It seemed so long since she'd been home. She was their daughter, but not the same woman who'd been taken from here only a few months ago. The changes would be hard for them to accept. She still struggled to believe it had all happened, and she lived through it.

"I've missed you both." Ella glanced at each of her parents. "Holding onto the faith I would be back here again one day kept me going. You may find this an odd statement but I'm glad I had the opportunity to discover everything I did. I would not have chosen to go through it all, but if I hadn't, I would've never discovered the truth about my birth parents, or that I have a sister. This will be tough for you both to understand, but as we tell the story, I hope you see that God truly works all things for our good."

Anna's eyes grew wide. "You have a sister? I can't wait to hear it all."

Shane loaded their bags in the back of the wagon.

Joshua helped Anna into the wagon next to him. Ella, Susie, and Shane sat in the back. As they traveled the dusty road, it wasn't long before Susie's head fell forward. She'd fallen asleep. Oh, to have the concerns of a child. Although, as an orphan herself, Ella understood Susie's troubles had been many.

Shane grabbed Ella's hand, and she slipped her fingers through his. They'd grown even closer in the last few weeks as they'd settled things in Cripple Creek, traveled to Denver, and stayed with Shane's parents while his father wrapped up the loose ends.

Ella laid her head against Shane's shoulder. The next few hours would be crucial first steps in hopes of everyone giving him a chance. They hoped to have an actual wedding with all the family to make their marriage feel legitimate. Before long, she'd followed Susie's lead to the land of slumber.

~

Shane gently shook Ella's shoulder. "I think we're here."

Ella sat up. They stopped in front of a two-story

farmhouse. Grandma Clara rocked in the porch swing watching Ella's siblings Seth, Rebecca, Emily and James run around while she held baby Noah. Luke and Megan sat next to Clara while their two-year-old twins, Ben and Rachel struggled to keep up with the older children. Wesley and Sophie watched their six-month-old son, Matthew, crawl around the porch. Wesley's sister, Katie, sat on the steps by herself. At fifteen, she no longer wanted to run with the younger children. She had a puppy nestled in her lap. Yelling and giggles filled the air. Home brought peace to Ella's bruised heart.

Shane helped Ella and Susie out of the wagon. Joshua did the same for Anna. They were greeted by shouts of, "They're here," as the children ran over and hugged Ella then stared at Shane and Susie.

Ella smiled at everybody. "I'd like everyone to meet my husband, Shane, and this sweet girl is, Susie." Surprised looks radiated from the older children. They will be staying here with us.

"That's yet to be determined." Ella heard her father say under his breath.

Clara stood up with the baby. "Supper is ready. I'm sure everyone wants to hear Ella's story, but I think we should eat first."

The children giggled. Ella, Shane, and Susie lagged behind everybody as they filed into the house. The meal couldn't have been more delicious and their conversations centered on matters that had been taking place on the farm, along with the children's funny escapades.

When they'd finished, the children settled down

to play games, read books and make up exciting adventures. The adults sat around the porch listening to the crickets chirp while sipping their coffee and tea.

Anna scooted to the edge of her chair. "So, Mr. Wyatt, one day Ella left to go take care of the horses on a neighboring farm. Later, we're told she didn't show up. We discovered evidence of a skirmish which took place on the road she traveled. We were praying for the best but had no idea who'd do such a thing. We sent telegrams to neighboring towns with a description of Ella, but no one saw her. A few days later we received the first telegram from her, stating she was all right and would be in touch again. Of course, Joshua headed to Dallas. People at the telegraph office said they remembered her, but had no idea what train she'd left on. A couple of weeks later, we got another telegram from Ella telling us that she was contacted by a private investigator... I assume that's you, Mr. Wyatt... who was taking her to meet her birth mother. We were happy for her, and somewhat at ease, until she sent us a couple more telegrams from Denver hinting that her life had been in peril and she didn't initially leave of her own free will.

Joshua glared at Shane, his brows furrowed as he spoke. "I expect you understand how painful this has been on us, Mr. Wyatt. If you had good intentions, why did you force Ella to go? We assume you meant her no harm, but yet, you were the one who put her life in danger." Any tension that had dissipated between Joshua and Shane at dinner, had now returned.

"Yes, I'm the one you should blame. I forced Ella to come with me because I needed to collect my fee from her mother, who'd contracted me to take Ella to her. My life and my family member's lives were being threatened because of gambling debts I owed to some dangerous men. Her mother said Ella had been taken from her as a baby. She'd employed some detectives to locate her. Once they found her, she hired me to get her to Colorado. I'd never taken anyone by force before, but I hoped in time I could convince Ella I was doing a good deed by reuniting them. I never planned on hurting her in any way."

Joshua stood up. "Didn't you consider taking her from her family hurting her?"

Shane glanced at Ella. "You're right. I only thought of myself. If I could go back and do it again, I wouldn't have kidnapped her. I would've explained everything to all of you and informed you what I'd been hired to do."

Ella butted in. "Father, as you can imagine, I was scared at the beginning. Even though Shane said he didn't want to hurt me, I wasn't sure what he might do. He kept my hands tied most of the time, but he never harmed me in any way." Shane saved me from being raped and most likely killed by an outlaw. He had left me tied to a tree outside of town while he rode for food and supplies. This outlaw found me and wanted to take me to his gang, but not before beating and raping me. Thank God, Shane got back in time and killed him. That was a turning point for me. He had tried to persuade me to go willingly, and through our conversations, I finally believed he might be telling the truth. So I agreed to go and not run away.

Shane and Ella continued telling her parents about the struggles they faced together on their journey. From the devastating tornado that took many lives on the train, and left Susie without anyone, to their time in Denver with Shane's family, when they realized they cared for each other. Joshua paced the porch mumbling.

"The rest of the story may be painful for you all to hear, so bear with us as we get through it, and remember we're all fine." Ella glanced at her mother.

"You mean it gets worse." She sat back in her chair.

"Yes," Ella said as she watched her father shake his head and continue to pace.

Shane coughed nervously, then took a gulp of coffee.

"When we arrived in Cripple Creek, Shane took me to meet my birth mother, Belle. Shane had kept her identity a secret from me. She was the madam of a rather large brothel. She'd been a prostitute in her teens and then a madam but found out there was lots more money to be made in the mining towns out west. She moved to Colorado and opened her bordello." Ella told them the entire story of how Belle's parents died and then she'd gotten dragged into prostitution and given drugs at fourteen and had stayed on them until a few years ago. How Ella's father rescued Belle from prostitution, and two years later, she left him. Which led to him leaving Ella at an orphanage.

Time went from minutes to an hour as they continued to tell what took place. Joshua had finally sat down. They recounted how they got drawn into the battle between Janson and Belle. She'd told Ella she was dying and wanted to make matters right with Ella before she died. Ella went into the part of the story where Janson threatened all their lives, and how she met Pastor Harris when they'd sent a telegram to Shane's father.

Ella continued the story telling them everything from how she got captured spying at Janson's house, to the elaborate plan of murdering his business partner and framing it on Belle. She teared up when she told about Janson shooting at Ella, but Belle saved her. One of Belle's men killed Janson.

"Pastor Harris helped get Belle to the carriage. Before she died, she recognized him, and told me he was my birth father. They'd never divorced, and he'd moved to Colorado to build a new life. In her last minutes, Belle asked for forgiveness not only from us but from Jesus." Ella's voice cracked. Her eyes wet with emotion remembering the woman who gave her life, but she never had the chance to know.

"Her funeral was beautiful. God used Pastor Harris to turn a day of mourning into a day of celebration because Shane and others at the funeral surrendered their hearts to God." Joshua and Anna glanced at Shane, who wiped the corners of his eyes with his finger as Ella described that day.

She continued. "A few days later I recalled her saying right she'd hidden a box. We discovered it in a magnificent garden she'd created across the alley from the brothel and behind stone walls. It was incredible to see such a beautiful place in the midst of that dirty and sin-filled mining town. Inside the box were the deeds to her properties and a letter Belle wrote. The letter explained who she wished her estate to go to, and most incredibly, I found out I have a sister in New York City. Belle had been pregnant when she'd left Pastor Harris. She hired someone to take care of, Sara, my sister until she was old enough to put into boarding schools. She visited her whenever she could. Sara isn't aware of what our mother did for work, that her father is alive, or that she has a sister.

Pastor Harris is traveling to New York to tell Sara about Belle. He took the letter from her with him so he could prove he's her father. Before he left, Pastor Harris tearfully informed me he'd left me at the orphanage because he couldn't find a job and didn't want to see me hungry any longer. He moved west to find work and drove cattle until it became too physically painful for him. He ended up in Cripple Creek and found Belle by accident. She'd been sitting at a park when he first saw her.

It hurt him to find out she owned a brothel. He drank a lot and almost died in a fight with another man. Hungover, he stumbled into a church the next morning and that's when God transformed his life. He decided to become a pastor. He wanted to bring me out to Colorado and wrote The Children's Aid Society, but they told him I'd went west on an orphan train. Their records stated a family in Texas adopted me, so he chose not to disrupt my life. He hopes we can all be a part of each other's lives."

Ella stood up. "No one will ever replace any of you, but I know you all will understand I need to spend time with them if they move here."

The sounds of Crickets chirping and owls hooting met the end of Ella's story. Sophie stood and hugged her. "Oh my dear, you've been through so much. This is unbelievable. Your head must still be reeling." She looked over at Shane. "I'm glad you straightened your life out and brought her back to us unharmed. But, part of me wonders if you're really the changed man you and Ella say you are. It may take some time for you to show us you are that guy. I love this woman as a sister."

"Shane and I are married. What I wish for is a wedding here with all my family in a few weeks so we can begin a life together. Ella made eye contact with everyone. He has more than proven himself to me. I love him."

Shane stood and pulled Ella close to his side. "I told her that some of you might want me to go to jail. I hurt everyone who loves her. Sorry isn't enough, nor does it change the facts, but I am absolutely ashamed that I endangered Ella's life. Good has come from all of this. Ella would have never known her birth mother and father, and why they did what they did. She wouldn't know she has a sister. And this may be selfish, but I wouldn't have been blessed with having this beautiful woman as my wife. I love her with all my heart and will spend the rest of my life making it up to her and all of you."

Clara walked over and hugged Ella. "You know how much I love you. If you think Shane is the man

God has for you, then I trust your judgment, but you'll have to give us time to see it in him. Clara sat back down and pulled a blanket around her."

"Words are easy. I hope for Ella's sake what's been said is true. It crushes my heart to realize Ella could have been killed multiple times, and I wasn't there for her. If I'd had any idea where you all were, I would've ridden there and brought her home. Your choices almost took from me one of the most precious gifts God gave me." Joshua's voice got louder. "It's hard for me to even look at you, much less let you stand next to my daughter. I want Ella to return to her room in the house. You can sleep in the bunkhouse and work with the ranch hands. You can eat your dinners in our home, the other meals with the men. After dinner, you and Ella can spend a couple of hours together around the rest of us. If you don't like these arrangements, then you should get on the next train to Denver and we'll have this marriage annulled. If at any point I'm not happy with your work or how you treat Ella you'll be on the first train out of here. Report to Wesley first thing in the morning. If I put you under Luke he might kill you, so be grateful Wesley will give you a fair shake." Joshua walked into his home, letting the screen door slam behind him.

Ella's heart sank, tears rolled down her cheeks. She turned her face into Shane's side. Hadn't they been through enough?

Luke walked over to them. "Joshua's right. I've loved this gal like my own sister ever since she and her mother showed up at the ranch. But, I see how much she loves you. We'll all be fair with you,

Shane, which is more than you probably deserve. We're going to take the twins home and put them to bed. I'll talk with you in the morning before you ride out with Wesley." Luke hugged Ella. "Glad you're safe and home."

Wesley picked up his son and stared at Shane. "Meet me out in front of the barn before the sun is up. We need to get our little guy to bed. I'll tell the men you'll be staying in the bunkhouse. Ella can show you where it is when you're ready."

Ella and Shane sat down as everybody left to go to their homes. Clara took Ella's siblings inside. Only Anna remained.

"How do you feel about all that was said, Ella?"

"I don't think everyone understands how much we've been through and we're ready to begin our life together. I understand why Father is upset but I'm an adult and married." Ella glanced at Shane.

"You're right. The two of you could leave and start living your life, you are adults. Joshua and I have been extremely worried and upset over this and we didn't even guess the half of it. Hearing all you've been through broke our hearts and made us realize how close we came to losing you. If you do things the way your father wants you to and Shane proves himself, it may take a while longer to be together, but when you do, it'll be so much better because you'll have our blessing."

"If I had a daughter, I couldn't see myself being any different. Working here to show I'm worthy to have Ella as my wife is not asking too much." Shane grabbed Ella's hand. "You all are hearing this story for the first time and need a while to sort it out."

"Mother, once I found out this woman could be my birth mother, there was a part of me hoping it was true. I needed to understand why my parents didn't keep me. Shane may have forced me to go at the beginning, but before we even got on the train to Denver, I'd decided I was going."

"I understand why you would feel that way, Ella. I would've wanted to know as well. Ultimately, if Shane is who God intended for you, then no one will be against that."

Anna turned toward Shane. "If you work with integrity around here, the reward will far exceed the wait."

"Your room is ready for you, Ella. Please show Shane where the bunkhouse is. Good night." Anna went inside.

Chapter Twenty

"Let's walk down to the lake." Ella grabbed Shane's arm and pulled him along.

"Are you sure we're allowed?" Shane laughed.

"Those rules don't start until tomorrow." Ella took off running.

Shane stayed close behind her. "I hope you're right."

They sat on the big flat rock Ella had loved since her mother married Joshua. They watched the reflection of the moon shimmering on the water's ripples. She wasn't happy with her father's reaction and the rules he imposed on Shane. She understood why but it didn't make it easy for them when they'd been through so much already. She hoped he would give Shane a fair chance.

They sat in silence, each caught up in their own thoughts of what might happen from here.

Shane rubbed his thumb over the top of her hand. "So does this Clint guy have a chance of changing your mind?"

"No. I don't want to hurt him, but I don't love him. I love you, Mr. Wyatt. Who would've even dreamed that might be possible?"

"I'm glad you don't love him. I didn't want to have to take you captive again." Shane entwined his fingers with Ella's.

"You captured my heart when you showed me who you could be. Are you up to the task of winning my father's approval?"

"I'm sure none of them will make it easy for me, but knowing you're my reward if I succeed, I won't fail. I have God on my side now. I'm not doing it alone."

"How long do you think before we can be husband and wife for real?"

"With a little incentive, we can have that wedding in a couple of months." Shane winked at her.

"What would be an incentive for you?"

"Maybe a kiss now and then."

"I don't think that's on the approved list."

"Walks to the lake alone at night probably aren't on the list either, yet you dragged me here." Shane smiled.

"Dragged you here? Why, Mr. Wyatt, did I take you against your will?" Her long eyelashes fluttered, as she gazed into his eyes.

"I'd go with you anywhere, Mrs. Wyatt. Anytime I can be alone with you, holding your hand, is where I choose to be. What more do I need?"

"Maybe a kiss?" Ella lightly kissed Shane's lips.

"Is that all?"

"Well, someone might be watching."

Shane brushed his lips against hers "You said it didn't start until tomorrow." She waited for him to kiss her but he didn't.

"Really?"

"Yep. That's as far as it goes."

"You're not getting away with that." Ella pulled him closer and kissed him lovingly. They lost track of time as the ugliness of the last few weeks faded. Nothing felt better than to be in his embrace, with his kisses leaving her breathless.

"We should stop. You've persuaded me that even though we're already married, I should do everything I can to make that wedding day get here as soon as possible. I'll do whatever it takes to show your father I'm worthy of you. You've taken my heart captive, my beautiful red-haired angel. I love you, Ella Wyatt."

"I love you too, Shane Wyatt. We've conquered much harder challenges together, and we will win my father over too."

"I sure hope so." Shane took her hand. "Better take me to that bunkhouse. I'm confident the men are waiting to make life miserable for me."

The End

DARLIA SAWYER

Darlia Sawyer Biography

Darlia Sawyer grew up living in many of the western states during her childhood. She now lives in Western Colorado and considers it to be a blessing. Beautiful scenery, rich history and great weather to enjoy it all in.

She lost her husband of twenty years in 2004 after dealing with medical issues his whole life. Her relationship with Jesus and her daughter and two sons helped her through those days.

She married Ken in 2007 and together they have three boys and three girls, just like the Brady Bunch. All the children are now adults and they've added two son-in-law's, three adorable granddaughters and a grandson to the family. This year we'll be adding a daughter-in-law.

There have always been two constants in her life. The love and strength found in her relationship with her Heavenly Father and her love for writing and history.

The support from her husband, Ken, has given her the opportunity to follow her lifelong dream of writing full time.

She hopes her writing will inspire hope, a passion for life and the chance to once again believe in miracles.

Please follow her on the following social media links:

https://amazon.com/author/darliasawyer

https://www.facebook.com/DarliaSawyerAuthor

https://twitter.com/DarliaSawyer

https://www.instagram.com/darliasawyer

https://www.goodreads.com/author/show/16670538.Darlia_Sawyer

https://www.pinterest.com/darlias/

If you liked *A Captive Heart* please leave a review on Amazon. The release of *A Forgiving Heart* will be out in the near future.

If you haven't read the first two books in the series, *A Home for Her Heart* and *A Healing Heart* please check them out on Amazon.

Keep reading for the first chapter of *A Home for Her Heart*.

DARLIA SAWYER

A Home for Her Heart

Chapter One

1891

Tears spilled down Ella's cheeks as Anna Wilson helped her step off the orphan train in Longview, Texas. She embraced the twelve-year-old girl. "What's wrong, Ella? Are you tired? I would understand if you were. We've traveled to so many towns in the last several weeks."

Ella wiped tears from her eyes. "No one wants me."

"I'm trying my best to find homes for each of you. You all deserve to have the love of a family." Anna hugged the six children in her care. "I have a good feeling about today. The last agent said several families' were waiting for the next orphan train."

Anna noticed Ella's flushed cheeks "Ella, you look warm. Are you running a temperature?"

"I don't think so." Ella pulled at the front of her dress. "It's hot."

"This Texas humidity is suffocating." Anna laid her hand on Ella's forehead. "You're not running a temperature. I hope the people today understand what gifts each of you are. We're late, let's go find the opera house."

Anna followed the six children along the wooden sidewalk. Ella's red curls bounced with each step she took. Dust engulfed them from the passing horses and wagons. Michael coughed. *Did anyone ever get used to all this dirt?* Anna understood now why they covered the streets in New York with brick. It made walking so much easier. They passed by a bakery and the aroma of homemade bread made Anna's mouth water.

"I'm hungry. Can we buy sweet rolls, Miss Wilson?" Sam asked.

"I wish we had time. They smell wonderful." Anna spotted the opera house across the street. "We're almost there."

Anna opened the door of a two-story brick building and they walked in. Their train had arrived an hour late, and there were around twenty people waiting for them. There were more women than men sitting in groups and talking. A middle-aged man in a black suit came toward them.

"Welcome. I'm Pastor Williams and we've been expecting you." He held his hand out to Anna. "Did everyone have a pleasant trip?" He didn't wait for the children to respond. He asked Anna. "Are you comfortable introducing yourself?"

She shook his hand. "Yes to both questions and thank you. Children, please go sit in the chairs they've set out on stage."

Anna followed the children down the aisle, admiring the stained-glass windows of the Longview Opera House. There were four long windows on each side, and they cast shades of yellow, red, green and blue on the wooden floor in a kaleidoscope of colors. Each window depicted a scene from a famous play. It reminded Anna of the church her parents attended when she was a little girl. She hadn't been to church since then. Grief caught Anna by surprise and she had a difficult time holding back tears. Her parents had died eight years ago.

Her heart broke for each child on stage. Most of them had never known their parents, and the rest had lost theirs at a young age. The orphanage had provided the girls with white dresses, stockings, shoes and a bow. The four boys had on white shirts, jackets, knee pants, hats, socks and shoes. They looked adorable. Their sole possessions included one more outfit and a Bible.

Anna stepped to the front of the stage. She no longer got nervous speaking in front of people. Her concern for the children pushed her to overcome the anxiousness she used to feel.

"I want to thank everyone for coming. My name is Anna Wilson. I am an agent for the Children's Aid Society in New York City. We have traveled many miles to find families who will love these children. I care about each of them."

"They listen well and are considerate and loving. In the past, many people thought it appropriate to treat orphans as servants. I won't allow this." Anna glared at the audience. "I hope you'll love them as your own. Most of them were living on the streets before someone took them to the Children's Aid Society. They'd lost one or both parents and often their siblings. Their lives have been filled with difficulties and sorrow. My hope is you'll find it a privilege to provide a home for them. In return they'll show you how much it means to be a part of your family."

"When I finish speaking, I hope you'll talk with each child. I have a few rules," Anna studied the crowd. "I don't allow anyone to touch their muscles or look at their teeth. They're all healthy. Agents used to allow this, but I won't. They need respect. If you're interested in a child, I'll check with Longview's community leaders to find out if they believe your family would provide a good home. The children must feel comfortable around you, so I'll watch how you communicate and connect with them." She cleared her throat. "Could we get a drink of water? We had a long train ride and we're not used to this heat."

Pastor Williams left and returned with a bucket of water and a ladle.

"Thank you." Anna let the children drink first. She wished they had ice for the warm water, but it eased her parched throat.

"I'd like to introduce everyone. Children, please step forward when I say your name. First is Sam Foster, he's twelve." A lanky brown haired boy took his place by Anna. "A family in Opelousas, Louisiana took his younger brother Ben. They didn't have room for both boys. Sam has Ben's address so he can write to him. He wants to visit him one day. Their parents died in a factory fire. When Sam was eight and Ben was five, someone found them on the streets and brought them to the orphanage."

"Next is Ella Murphey, she's twelve." Ella stood next to Sam. She was taller than him and her red curls stuck out in every direction. Her cheeks grew pink which caused her freckles to appear darker. "Ella helps with the little ones. I don't know what I would've done without her. She doesn't remember her family. Her father brought her to the orphanage when she was three."

"Then we have Matthew, he's ten." He tried to go on the opposite side of Miss Wilson but Ella grabbed his arm and pulled him beside her. Matthew frowned at Ella but recovered quickly and turned toward the audience and smiled, causing dimples to appear in his chubby cheeks. "His parents and siblings died from typhoid. A couple found him huddled in a corner of the apartment building they'd lived in and took him to the orphanage."

Anna motioned to the small blonde-haired girl to stand next to her. "Laura is eight. When her parents didn't return from a voyage to England, her grandmother cared for her. No one ever heard what happened to her parents. When her grandmother died Laura was only four. A family friend brought her to the orphanage."

"Last are five-year-old twins, Scott and Michael." They ran next to Laura. Each brother a mirror image of the other, black short hair, bright blue eyes and two missing top teeth. "If you're thinking about taking them, I hope you'll take both. Twins have a special connection. Their mother left them on the steps of the orphanage when they were babies. She'd pinned a note stating their names, and that she had no other choice. Thank you children, you can sit down. Does anyone have questions before you talk with them?" Anna watched a man get up and walk out. He wore torn jean overalls, and a ripped shirt. She wondered how often he bathed as there were dirt smudges across his face.

A woman with thick glasses stood up as she squinted at Anna. "If you're not married can you care for a child?"

Anna scanned the crowd. She guessed most of them to be in their late twenties or early thirties, including the woman asking the question. "We prefer you're married, but if you want to care for a child, we're willing to let you try."

A man in a gray vest, jacket, matching trousers and black top hat stood, "Do you check on each child after they go with a family? What if a child is unhappy and doesn't want to stay in your home? Or if the families realize they can't care for them, how would you resolve it?"

"Yes, agents check on the children each time they bring new orphans. I'll be here for two weeks to make sure they're adjusting well and to make sure children from previous orphan trains are doing well. The agent after me should do the same. If a child is unhappy, we find another family for them. If we can't, we take them back to the Children's Aid Society in New York City. Children have run away from homes, and we've never heard from them again. We often learn afterward that those children were being physically or emotionally mistreated." Anna patted Scott's shoulder as he hopped from one foot to the other.

An older woman in the back row covered her mouth with her gloved hand. "Oh my, who would do such awful things?"

"Sometimes a neighbor or family member will do things in the privacy of their home you'd never imagine. I hope if you notice or hear something bad happening in a family, you'll report it. I'm glad most problems we have aren't so awful and are easily worked out." Anna paused and tucked a few loose strands of her toffee brown hair behind her ear. "Anyone else?" No one spoke. "If you come up with other questions, I'd love to answer them. Thank you for coming."

Anna paced the stage as people came to talk with the children. It'd be difficult to let any of the children go. She'd come to love them. She walked over and stood in front of the curtain on the right side of the stage. She needed to get her emotions under control. Anna heard whispering behind her.

"Mary, what about the two girls?" A hoarse voice asked.

Anna noticed a hole in the curtain. She could see two older women through it.

"I'm not sure about the little girl, Bertha. The taller girl with red hair appears adequate." Mary glanced at the girls. "No one is saying anything to her, so you might be her only opportunity."

"I don't have time for nonsense. I need someone to do the housework I can no longer do. My health makes it difficult for me. I'm too old to take care of a child." Bertha sat in a wooden chair. It groaned and creaked beneath her. "She would have to follow my rules."

"Bertha, if she's in school, she can only help you in the evenings. And all children misbehave. I wonder if you have sufficient patience to have a child around, even an older one. Maybe this isn't the best solution for you." Mary sat next to her, clutching a big bag to her bosom.

"She doesn't need more school. She'll get real life experience taking care of a home. If she marries, she will need to know household management." Bertha scooted back in her chair, a snap caused her to stand abruptly, as the chair broke into pieces all over the floor. "They sure don't make chairs like they used to."

Anna had heard enough. She went around the curtain. "I overheard your conversation, and I won't let Ella leave with you. As I expressed in my introduction, they're not servants. They need love and a family. Ella is a lovely and helpful girl. She deserves more than someone who wants a housekeeper. You should both leave."

"Of all the nerve. Mary, let's go." Bertha's face turned red. "The mayor will hear about this. I wanted to help that child, and this is how I'm treated." Bertha waddled down the stairs, huffing and puffing her way through the people and out the door. Mary followed behind her.

Anna's heart raced as she walked back to the front of the stage. Her nails dug into her palms as she clenched her hands into fists. Her cheeks were on fire and she knew her face was red. *I can't believe how selfish people are. Ella deserves a real family.*

The well-dressed man who had asked the questions earlier approached Anna. He was holding hands with an attractive women. "Miss Wilson, my name is Thomas Gage, and this is my wife, Emma." He shook Anna's hand. "We're interested in providing a home for the twins. In our five years of marriage we haven't been blessed with children. Our home is nice and we have four bedrooms. I'm the town doctor and my wife would stay with them."

Anna drew a deep breath. "I appreciate you wanting to provide a home for them but are you aware of how rambunctious two little boys can be? They might destroy something valuable. If you had children of your own, would you still want the twins? Or would they be a burden to you?" Anna glared at Emma.

"Oh no, Miss Wilson, we'd think of the boys as ours." Mrs. Gage paused. "They'd be the older siblings to any child we might have. Once you give a child your heart, you wouldn't take it back. I assure you, God gives us enough love for everyone in our lives." She clutched her husband's hand as if clinging to a lifeline.

"I wonder if God bothers with such matters. He allowed their parents to give them away." Anna took a few deep breaths, to calm herself down. "I'm sorry if I sound cynical. Before I came over here, I overheard a conversation which upset me. My recommendation would be to take Michael and Scott for two hours today. When you're done, bring them to our hotel and you can do the same for the next few days. You could increase the time you have them each day. As long as everything goes well for the twins and both of you, we'll talk about a permanent arrangement." Anna smiled.

Mrs. Gage's expression softened. "Oh, what a wonderful idea. It'd give us time to get our home prepared." She glanced up at her husband. "What do you think, Thomas?"

"It's a good plan. We'll get to know them and they can decide if they want to live with us. Would it be all right if we took them to lunch and to our house to play? We have a large yard and a new furry puppy." Mr. Gage lifted his hat and wiped his forehead with a handkerchief.

"Let me talk with the boys. I'll be right back." Anna walked over to Michael and Scott. "There's a couple who wishes to have lunch with you both. After eating they'll take you to their home to play with their new puppy for a while. Would you like to go with them?"

"Yes, Miss Wilson," Michael gave her a toothless smile.

Scott nodded. "I would love to play with a puppy."

"When you are through playing, they'll bring you to the hotel. You'll have lots of fun." Anna walked back with the boys to give the good news to

Mr. and Mrs. Gage.

~

"Well girls, let's eat supper and find our hotel. Our luggage should be there." Anna took each girl by the hand. "I can't say I'm sorry the right family didn't come for you both. Now I have more time with you. We'll stay here for two weeks. Our next and last stop will be in Nacogdoches, Texas. I believe families are waiting there for both of you."

"It's all right Miss Wilson. No one wants me. They don't even speak to me. I'll go back to the orphanage with you." Ella wiped tears away.

"No one wants me either. They only take boys. I'm happy Sam, Matthew and the twins found families but why don't they like girls, Miss Wilson?" Laura looked up at Anna with her big blue eyes brimming with unshed tears. "Doesn't God want us to find a family?"

Anna's heart broke. The girls' lives had been full of disappointments. Every time she paraded them in front of families, their hopes were high they'd find a home. When they didn't, rejection and disappointment settled on them.

Anna understood their responses. She'd experienced pain when the man she'd loved rejected her for someone else. At twenty-nine her prospects of finding love were slim. She resented the label of spinster, but it applied to her. Anna wanted a family but how could she ever trust a man with her heart again?

She needed a plan to take care of these precious

girls. Ella's chances of someone wanting her for more than a housekeeper or nanny weren't good, as Anna had witnessed today. Laura wasn't as old, but girls weren't valued as highly as boys. The West needed laborers. Boys grew up and helped on the homesteads.

"Oh girls, you're beautiful. If the right family comes along, they'll love you as much as I do. I'm certain God wants you both to find families. Why wouldn't He? You're angels. After supper let's eat ice cream. It's been a long day and you both deserve a treat." Anna bent and wiped the tears away and kissed them on the cheek. "No more crying. It's time for fun."

Ella hugged Anna tight. "I wish we could stay with you, Miss Wilson."

"Me too." Laura joined in the hug.

"Me too." Anna whispered to herself.

~

The rocking rhythm of the train lolled Ella and Laura to sleep for most of the journey from Longview to Nacogdoches, Texas. Anna enjoyed looking out the window as forests and lakes sped by. She caught a whiff of coffee brewing in the dining car. Her stomach rumbled.

"Next stop Nacogdoches. Please prepare to disembark." The conductor announced.

Being an agent gave Anna the ability to travel and see places, but it didn't pay enough for her to live on her own. Maybe she should check into getting a teaching certificate and moving out West with the girls to teach.

Screeches and squeals from the train brakes startled Anna from her thoughts, and she looked outside at the depot coming into view.

Ella sat up, rubbing her eyes. "Are we there?"

"I believe so. We'll pick up our baggage and go to the hotel. I didn't know when we'd arrive when I sent out the telegram, so we won't be meeting with families until tomorrow." Anna stood. The girls followed her down the aisle.

"What a beautiful town." Anna glanced around at the small crowd as she stepped off the train. The smell of pine filled the air and evergreen trees stood as strong sentinels overlooking the area.

"It's pretty, Miss Wilson, so many trees. It's hot here too, but I like it. There's lots of shade." Ella stepped off the train.

Anna helped Laura down the steps. "Do you like it?"

"I do." Laura grabbed Ella's hand and smiled. "We'll meet our families here, Ella."

Ella stared at the ground. "You will, Laura."

"We need to get our luggage and find the hotel." Anna stepped backward and tripped over a satchel on the ground behind her. She tried regaining her balance, but instead strong arms wrapped around her waist. However, they didn't stop her fall. She landed on top of a muscular man.

"Oh my," Anna tried to push herself up. *Where should she place her hands so she wouldn't touch the man underneath her?* Her cheeks were on fire and people were starring.

"Miss Wilson, are you okay? That sure was funny," Ella giggled. "Grab my hands and I'll pull you up."

Anna made it to her feet and straightened her skirt. She turned around to thank the man who broke her fall. He wore jeans, brown cowboy boots and a white shirt. Dark brown hair waved from under his white cowboy hat. When she found the courage to look into his face, a pair of ice-blue eyes looked amused at her embarrassment. "I'm so sorry. I didn't check behind me before I backed up," she stammered. "Did I hurt you?"

"I'm fine, miss. Someone as slim as you wouldn't hurt me. I tried catching you but it didn't go as intended. Are you all right?" He held out his hand. "My name is Joshua."

Anna shook his hand. "I'm Anna Wilson and nothing is hurt, thanks to you. Glad you didn't hurt your head or break anything."

Joshua picked up the satchel. "It's dented. Is it yours?"

"It isn't. I wonder who'd sit a bag down and walk off?" Anna scanned the crowd, but no one rushed to claim the satchel. "I guess we should leave it, in case they come back. Do you know if they're unloading the luggage yet?"

Joshua sat the satchel on the ground. "We can find out. I need to get my mother's trunks. Follow me and I'll load your bags into your wagon."

"Oh, I wouldn't want to bother you with our bags. I'm sure you're busy, and we don't have a wagon. I'll hire someone to take our bags to the Grand Hotel." Anna took the girl's hands. "We'll follow you, though."

"It's no problem. I'll load your bags into my wagon and drop them off at the hotel. Which ones are yours? I'd offer you all a ride, but I'm out of room. My mother is coming to live with me and she brought enough trunks to fill two wagons. Which won't leave space for young ladies, sorry to say."

Anna tried to keep up with him. "Please don't bother about us. The girls and I like to walk. We'll get to see part of the town."

Joshua walked toward the men unloading luggage from the train to the wooden platform. He found his mother's trunks while Anna and the girls searched for theirs.

"We sat our luggage over there." Anna pointed to the bags. "Thank you again for helping us."

"You're welcome." Joshua smiled.

Anna's breath caught. Joshua had dimples, and his smile made her pulse pick up a beat or two. "Where is the Grand Hotel?"

"Turn right at the end of this street. It's three blocks down Main Street to the left. Have a good day ladies. It's nice to meet you." Joshua grabbed the bags.

"It was nice meeting you as well. Let's find the hotel, girls." Anna walked away but couldn't help taking one last glance at her rescuer. He was watching them. Their eyes met. Anna turned back around. *I'm sure he's married and has a family.*

She needed to accept her life. Her days would be filled with finding a home for the girls and checking on the children from previous orphan trains. Who had time for men, even the kind and handsome cowboy type men? He'd only end up breaking her heart.

www.ingramcontent.com/pod-product-compliance
Lightning Source LLC
LaVergne TN
LVHW010322070526
838199LV00065B/5629